The New York Times

BOOK OF
LIFETIME HISTORY

PERSONAL RECORDS

The New York Times

BOOK OF
LIFETIME HISTORY

PERSONAL
RECORDS

MARGARET ANN MARDEN

Times
BOOKS

Library of Congress Catalog Card Number: 77-79030

International Standard Book Number: 0-8129-0731-0

DESIGNED BY BETH TONDREAU
WITH ASSISTANCE FROM SHAREN DUGOFF

This Is a Personal Record

Given Name _____

FIRST   MIDDLE   LAST   MARRIED

Home Address at Time of Birth _____

STREET AND NUMBER

_____

CITY   STATE   ZIP

From Date	Subsequent Addresses	To Date

Table of Contents

PART IV: PROPERTY RECORDS

PART V: MISCELLANEOUS RECORDS AND LISTS

Preface

HAVE you had the experience of needing certain records and not having them available? On how many occasions have you needed to know your or your child's social security number? How often have you been confronted with forms requesting dates of immunizations and/or communicable diseases for your children? Most of us would like to get in the habit of keeping records for ourselves and our children. The format of this book is arranged so that an individual will have a source book for information about himself for a lifetime.

This book will be useful at school registration time and on other similar occasions. Take this book with you whenever you visit a clinic, doctor's or dentist's office. It is not necessary to record in detail the various findings on each physical, eye and dental examination. It *is* important to keep accurate records and to do so in a simple and concise way.

Young children need records kept for them because they will have no memory of events that happen early in their lives. If you are starting this book as an adult, fill in your past medical, eye and dental history as accurately as possible.

Legal records are absolutely essential to protect your estate. They must be kept accurately to be of any value to you. Take this book with you any time you consult a professional in legal matters.

Take this book with you when you are away on long trips. Emergencies arise at the most inconvenient times. These records will be valuable to you if you move or change doctors.

Medical personnel usually will not provide professional services without the patient's permission. In the case of minors, permission by the patient is legally inadequate. To prevent delay in care which might lead to complications it is strongly suggested that (in the absence of the parents or guardian) written consent for necessary emergency medical and surgical treatment be left with the person responsible for the individual. A suggested form to copy is included in the Medical Records section. Remember that you too are part of the decision making process and can expect in turn to be involved in "informed consent" with regard to medical procedures.

Each section of this book has been introduced by a leader in that field. An envelope has been provided at the back of the book for important papers. I hope that this concise personal record book will help you have an easier time with your record keeping.

MARGARET ANN MARDEN, R.N.

Acknowledgments

Introductions	Courtesy of:
Medical Records	Herbert A. Holden, M.D. Past President, American Academy of Family Physicians
Immunity Tests and Immunizations	Peter J. Leadley, M.D. Past Director of Health, State of Maine Department of Health and Welfare
Contagious Diseases	Merritt B. Low, M.D. Associate Director, and Head, Division of Chapters and Membership, American Academy of Pediatrics
Eye Records	Charles E. Jaeckle, M.D. Past President, American Association of Opthalmology
Dental Records	Copyright by the American Dental Association. Reprinted by permission.
Personal Records	James Brugler Bell Director and Librarian, New England Historic Genealogical Society
Legal Records	James D. Fellers, Esq. Past President, American Bar Association

Special thanks to:

Donald H. Marden, J.D.
Robert P. Dubord, D.M.D.
Beatrice Dubord
Judith H. Squire
Kevin Hill, M.D.
Edmund Ervin, M.D.
Emily Webster, R.N.
H. Sawin Millett, Jr.

Garrie J. Losee
Eugene Beaupre, M.D.
Bruce Olsen, Ph.D.
Wesley Mott, Ph.D.
Pamela J. Curtis
J. Lyle Conrad, M.D.
Judith L. Brody

Introduction

I'M at least as well organized as the next charlatan, which is the main reason why the paper work never gets more than—well—say several weeks ahead of me. The secret is that I've got a system. All of the papers get dumped on top of my dresser. When they've marinated for a week or so I go through them—usually on a Sunday afternoon, if I'm not playing tennis.

Lately I seem to have been playing a lot of tennis. Among the stuff in the marinade are dividend reinvestment statements from A.T. & T., General Electric, and General Motors. Any sensible person would long since have noted the contents of those statements in a permanent investment log—not only because it's nice to know how many shares of something you own, but because any sensible person would also realize that some of the information on the reinvestment statements is going to be needed for next year's tax statements.

The appeal of my system is that utility is never permitted to triumph over esthetics. It's the principle of double handling. Sifting through important papers three or four times a year—if they haven't dropped into total oblivion behind the dresser—gives them the kind of grungy patina that can't be touched by the precision of a single line entry in *The New York Times* PERSONAL RECORDS book.

That's clear from a couple of other papers I've just fished from the marinade—three statements from my broker that I'll have the pleasure of fondling again next tax time; a revised copy of a will that no executor would ever dream of looking for on the top of the dresser; a new American Express card whose number might some day find a permanent niche around here; and a receipted bill for $301.50 from Herb's Auto Body shop that I'd just as soon not talk about at all, except to note that it's grist for the tax mill, too.

I wouldn't mention any of this stuff, in fact, the detritus of a disorganized life, if I weren't so impressed with the organizing potential of this book. Inside every Chaos there's a Cosmos trying to break through.

The medical records alone are worth the price of entry. Not including myself, there are five children in the family. Over the years, the pediatrician has stuck them with more needles than Becton, Dickinson has syringes. The big questions are with what and when.

The when question surfaced the other day for about the fifteenth time when our daughter Sheila called from Philadelphia, where she is working for the summer. She's doing her junior year in college abroad, had just gotten her passport, and for her health form needed to know the date of her small pox immunization.

It's always nice to have a consultant around to handle the tough ones. I knew right off the date of Sheila's shot wasn't in the pile on the dresser. I try never to keep anything for as long as 20 years in the marinade, and Sheila, after all, had been stuck for the small pox when she was a wee tad.

"Where do we keep medical stuff?" I asked my wife.

"In the green box," she said, picking up the phone for another long distance chat with Sheila while I headed for the bedroom. That's where the green box is kept in a place of discreet honor on the top shelf of a closet.

The green box measures 9" x 7½" x 3½". It is leatherette, dates to the Pleistocene Era when somebody in the house used to buy Old Golds in Treasure Chest quantities, and is as fully packed as a Saratoga Trunk.

Rummaging through it in search of evidence that Sheila had indeed been pox-proofed, I found a number of records that should long since have made LIFETIME HISTORY. Among them were:
—An eagerly sought piece of paper announcing to the world that I, in 1946, had been honorably discharged from B Troop of the 43rd Cavalry Reconnaissance Squadron (Mechanized);
—An empty envelope from the Kentucky State Department of Health, postmarked April 3, 1956. It had once contained, I remembered, my wife's birth certificate—a certificate that had been obtained with great difficulty and the help of a brace of affidavits because some of the records in the small country town where she was born had somehow been irretrievably lost. Where was the certificate now I wondered?
—An envelope, also empty, marked "Tim's birth certificate." Still more wonder. Was there nothing official around to show that Timothy Phalon—fifth child, fourth son—was not a phantom in this vale of paperasserie?

The green box is packed with memories—a chunk of the long blonde pony tail, complete with rubber band, that Sheila wore before reaching for something more sophisticated at age seven; a kindergarten report card in which Miss Whalley praised Sheila's "happy disposition," but warned us that the kid, "in her enthusiasm tends to run instead of walk in the classroom."

Plenty of everything to conjure up sweetness past—hand crafted Christmas cards, a scrawl of Mother's Day notes—but no immunization card for Sheila.

There's something to be said for sentimental searches, but not when all you want is a simple, undiluted piece of information.

Fortunately, our pediatrician's records are organized, so Sheila was able to round out her health record after all. I intend to organize my records, too. That's why I've left the PERSONAL RECORDS where I know it can be found with no trouble at all—right on top of that pile of bumpf on the top of the dresser.

RICHARD PHALON

PART I
Beginnings

Genealogical Records

_____ | _____ | _____ | _____
_____ | _____ | _____ | _____
_____ | _____ | _____ | _____
_____ | _____ | _____ | _____

Great | Great | Great | Great
Grandmother | Grandfather | Grandmother | Grandfather

Grandmother | Grandfather

Mother

Child | Child | Child | Child

Spouse | Spouse | Spouse | Spouse

Grandchild | Grandchild | Grandchild | Grandchild

_____ | _____ | _____ | _____
_____ | _____ | _____ | _____

_____

_____

_____

_____

Genealogical Records

_____   _____   _____   _____

_____   _____   _____   _____

_____   _____   _____   _____

_____   _____   _____   _____

| Great Grandmother | Great Grandfather | Great Grandmother | Great Grandfather |

| Grandmother | Grandfather |

| Father |

Child	Child	Child	Child
Spouse	Spouse	Spouse	Spouse
Grandchild	Grandchild	Grandchild	Grandchild

_____   _____   _____   _____

_____   _____   _____   _____

_____

_____

_____

_____

Birth Records

Name _____
          FIRST   MIDDLE   LAST

Date of Birth _____
          MONTH   DAY   YEAR   TIME

Place of Birth _____
                     HOSPITAL OR HOME ADDRESS

_____
  STREET   CITY   COUNTY   STATE   ZIP

Mother's Maiden Name _____
                    FIRST   MIDDLE   LAST

Mother's Birthplace_____ Race_____

Father's Name _____
             FIRST   MIDDLE   LAST

Father's Birthplace_____ Race_____

Delivered by_____

Address _____

Named for_____

BIRTH CERTIFICATE INFORMATION

(A holder for a copy of the birth certificate is provided in the back of this book)

Certificate Kept or Filed at_____

_____
  STREET   CITY   COUNTY   STATE   ZIP

Date Recorded_____ Certificate Number_____

Legal Guardian, if any _____
                               NAME

_____
  STREET   CITY   COUNTY   STATE   ZIP

Adoption Records

Natural Parents _____

_____

Adoptive Parents_____

_____

Placement Date _____

Adoption Date_____

Name and Address of Court_____

_____

Name of Judge_____

Location of Adoption Records _____

_____

Agency_____

Address _____

_____

Remarks_____

_____

_____

_____

_____

_____

CHILDHOOD
GENERAL HEALTH

Delivery and Newborn Period

Mother's Health During this Pregnancy   Excellent___ Other___

(Describe) _____

_____

Duration of Pregnancy_____ Uneventful_____

Complicated by _____

Natural Delivery ___ Caesarean ___ Complications___ Uneventful ___

(Describe) _____

_____

Birth Weight_____lbs._____ozs. Birth Length_____inches

Sex   Male___ Female___

Condition of Baby at Birth _____

_____

Abnormalities or Diseases (present at time of birth)_____

_____

_____

_____

NEWBORN TESTS

Newborn Examination_____ _____
                            DATE   DOCTOR

Results _____

_____

_____

_____

PKU TESTS

Blood Date_____ Results_____ Urine Date_____ Results _____

BLOOD TESTS

Type of Test_____ Doctor _____

OTHER TESTS

Type of Test_____ Doctor _____

Date_____ Results _____

CIRCUMCISION

Date_____ Performed by _____

Hospital or Address _____

Comments_____

_____

_____

DISTINGUISHING FEATURES

	At Birth	Later	Date
Color of Eyes			
Color of Hair			
Color of Brows			
Color of Lashes			
Complexion			

Birthmarks	At Birth	Later

FEEDING SCHEDULE

	Date(s)	Comments
Breast Fed	_____	_____
		_____
Supplemented	_____	_____
		_____
Bottle Fed	_____	_____
		_____
Formula	_____	_____
	_____	_____
	_____	_____
	_____	_____
Feeding Intervals	_____	_____
	_____	_____
	_____	_____
	_____	_____
Weaning	_____	_____

Vitamins Prescribed	Date Started	Date Stopped
_____	_____	_____
_____	_____	_____
_____	_____	_____
_____	_____	_____

DIET

Diet	Date Started	Comments
Milk Formula	_____	_____
Strained Cereal	_____	_____
Strained Fruit	_____	_____
Strained Vegetables	_____	_____
Strained Meats	_____	_____
Juices _____	_____	_____
_____	_____	_____
_____	_____	_____
_____	_____	_____
Eggs	_____	_____
Bread	_____	_____
Fish	_____	_____

Other Firsts in Diet:

_____	_____	_____
_____	_____	_____
_____	_____	_____
_____	_____	_____
_____	_____	_____
_____	_____	_____

Developmental History

	Age
Eyes and head follow moving object	——
Smiles	——
Lifts head when lying	——
Grasps small object	——
Transfers object from one hand to other	——
Rolls from stomach to back	——
Rolls from back to stomach	——
Sits with help	——
Sits in a chair	——
Pulls self to standing position	——
Stands alone	——
Crawls	——
Walks with help	——
Walks alone	——
Repeats syllables (ma-ma, da-da)	——
Single words	——
Sentences of more than four words	——
Climbs stairs	——
Toilet training accomplished Day	——
Night	——
Preferred hand	——

Comments on any of the above_____

_____

_____

_____

_____

_____

_____

Childhood Weight
and Height Record

Age	Date	Weight	Height

Blood Group

The blood group should be recorded. It remains the same throughout life.

Blood Type_____ Rh Factor: Positive___ Negative___

RECORD OF BLOOD DONATIONS

Date	Blood Bank	Address

RECORD OF BLOOD TRANSFUSIONS RECEIVED

Date_____ Doctor_____

Address or Hospital_____

Number of Units Received_____

Remarks_____

Date_____ Doctor_____

Address or Hospital_____

Number of Units Received_____

Remarks_____

Date_____ Doctor_____

Address or Hospital_____

Number of Units Received_____

Remarks_____

Date_____ Doctor_____

Address or Hospital_____

Number of Units Received_____

Remarks_____

Family Medical History

Any disease that "runs in your family" should be discussed with your doctor.

	Father	Paternal Grandfather	Paternal Grandmother	Mother	Maternal Grandfather	Maternal Grandmother	Siblings					Spouse	Children					
Allergies																		
Amblyopia																		
Anemia																		
Asthma																		
Arthritis																		
Bladder or Kidney Trouble																		
Bleeding Tendencies																		
Cancer or Tumor																		
Diabetes																		
Epilepsy																		
Glaucoma																		
Gout																		
Hearing Defects																		
Heart Trouble																		
High Blood Pressure																		
Mental Illness																		
Mental Retardation																		
Rheumatism																		
Stomach or Duodenal Ulcer																		
Strabismus (Crossed Eyes)																		
Stroke																		
Tuberculosis																		
Other																		
Age at Death																		
General Health (Good or Poor)																		
BIRTH DATE																		

CHILDHOOD
DENTAL RECORDS

Primary Teeth

	Upper Left Eruption Date	Date Shed	Upper Right Eruption Date	Date Shed
1. Central incisors				
2. Lateral incisors				
3. Cuspids				
4. First molars				
5. Second molars				

	Lower Left Eruption Date	Date Shed	Lower Right Eruption Date	Date Shed
1. Central incisors				
2. Lateral incisors				
3. Cuspids				
4. First molars				
5. Second molars				

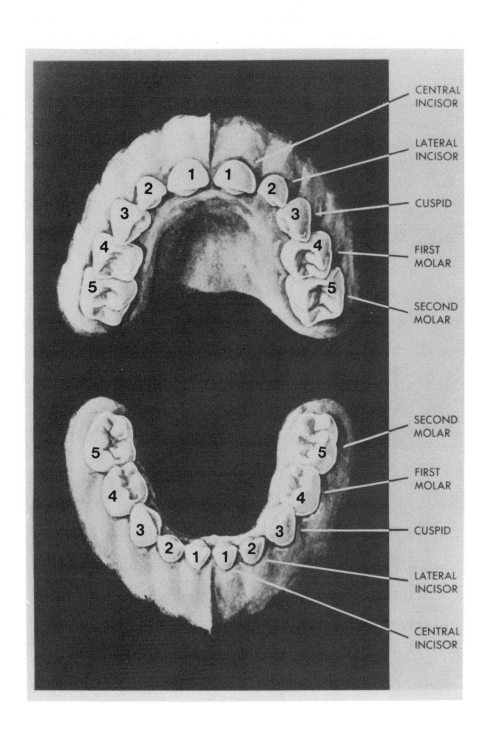

CENTRAL
INCISOR

LATERAL
INCISOR

CUSPID

FIRST
MOLAR

SECOND
MOLAR

SECOND
MOLAR

FIRST
MOLAR

CUSPID

LATERAL
INCISOR

CENTRAL
INCISOR

31

Childhood Dental Examinations

Date _____

Dentist _____

Address _____

Remarks _____

_____

_____

Date _____

Dentist _____

Address _____

Remarks _____

_____

_____

Date _____

Dentist _____

Address _____

Remarks _____

_____

_____

Date_____

Dentist_____

Address_____

Remarks_____

_____

_____

Date_____

Dentist_____

Address_____

Remarks_____

_____

_____

Date_____

Dentist_____

Address_____

Remarks_____

_____

_____

Date_____

Dentist _____

Address _____

Remarks_____

_____

_____

Date_____

Dentist _____

Address _____

Remarks_____

_____

_____

Date_____

Dentist _____

Address _____

Remarks_____

_____

_____

Orthodontia

Date_____

Orthodontist_____

Address_____

Work Done_____

_____

Work Needed_____

_____

Remarks_____

_____

Date_____

Orthodontist_____

Address_____

Work Done_____

_____

Work Needed_____

_____

Remarks_____

_____

Date _____

Orthodontist _____

Address _____

Work Done _____

_____

Work Needed _____

_____

Remarks _____

_____

_____

Date _____

Orthodontist _____

Address _____

Work Done _____

_____

Work Needed _____

_____

Remarks _____

_____

_____

Date

Orthodontist

Address

Work Done

Work Needed

Remarks

Date

Orthodontist

Address

Work Done

Work Needed

Remarks

Date _____

Orthodontist _____

Address _____

Work Done _____

_____

Work Needed _____

_____

Remarks _____

_____

_____

Date _____

Orthodontist _____

Address _____

Work Done _____

_____

Work Needed _____

_____

Remarks _____

_____

_____

Additional Record Space
For Beginnings

Additional Record Space
For Beginnings

Part II

Personal Records

Introduction

THE value of accurate personal records cannot be overestimated. In this mobile society of ours where an individual is frequently separated by great distance from his place of origin and upbringing, a personal file of vital information facilitates his entrance into a new community. For example, church membership files require information on birth, baptism, and confirmation. Employment applications ask for past job experiences (often including addresses) and educational data (beginning with high school). These records are equally useful in cases of serious illness or death, providing the family with the information necessary to apply for medical benefits, or, ultimately, to settle the deceased's estate. The importance of these records suggests that they should be accurately maintained throughout one's life.

JAMES BRUGLER BELL
Director and Librarian,
New England Historic Genealogical Society

Citizenship

Alien＿＿＿＿＿＿＿＿＿＿＿＿＿ Registration Number＿＿＿＿＿＿＿＿＿＿

Native Country ＿＿＿＿＿＿＿＿＿＿＿＿＿＿＿＿＿＿＿＿＿＿＿＿＿＿

Date and Port of Entry＿＿＿＿＿＿＿＿＿＿＿＿＿＿＿＿＿＿＿＿＿＿＿

Date of Naturalization ＿＿＿＿＿＿＿＿＿＿＿＿＿＿＿＿＿＿＿＿＿＿＿

Place of Naturalization＿＿＿＿＿＿＿＿＿＿＿＿＿＿＿＿＿＿＿＿＿＿＿

Location of Naturalization Records＿＿＿＿＿＿＿＿＿＿＿＿＿＿＿＿＿

Naturalization Certificate Number ＿＿＿＿＿＿＿＿＿＿＿＿＿＿＿＿＿

If Derived, Parents' Certificate Number(s) ＿＿＿＿＿＿＿＿＿＿＿＿

IDENTIFICATION

Fingerprints, palmprints, footprints, etc.
At birth or later in life

Date＿＿＿＿＿＿＿＿＿＿＿＿＿＿＿＿＿＿＿＿＿＿＿＿＿＿＿＿＿＿＿＿

Type of Identification＿＿＿＿＿＿＿＿＿＿＿＿＿＿＿＿＿＿＿＿＿＿＿

Person Making Identification＿＿＿＿＿＿＿＿＿＿＿＿＿＿＿＿＿＿＿

Location of Prints ＿＿＿＿＿＿＿＿＿＿＿＿＿＿＿＿＿＿＿＿＿＿＿＿

Immediate Family

Name   Birthday

_____   _____

_____   _____

_____   _____

_____   _____

_____   _____

_____   _____

_____   _____

_____   _____

_____   _____

_____   _____

_____   _____

_____   _____

_____   _____

_____   _____

_____   _____

Religious Affiliations

Religion _____

Religious Name_____ Named for _____

Godmother _____

Godfather _____

Baptism   Date_____ Where Certificate Kept _____

_____

Clergyman Officiating _____

Church_____

First Communion   Date_____ Where Certificate Kept_____

_____

Clergyman Officiating_____

Church_____

Confirmation   Date_____ Where Certificate Kept _____

_____

Clergyman Officiating_____

Church_____

Bar (Bat) Mitzvah   Date_____ Synagogue_____

Rabbi Officiating_____

Cantor Officiating_____

Remarks_____

OTHER CEREMONIES

_____

_____

_____

_____

_____

RELIGIOUS EDUCATION AND ACTIVITIES

_____

_____

_____

_____

_____

_____

_____

CHURCH/SYNAGOGUE MEMBERSHIP

Name _____

Address _____

Dates From-To_____

Name _____

Address _____

Dates From-To_____

Name _____

Address _____

Dates From-To_____

Name _____

Address _____

Dates From-To_____

Name _____

Address _____

Dates From-To_____

Education

Dates From-To _____

Name of School _____

Address _____

_____

Grade Completed or Degree _____

Remarks* _____

_____

Where Diploma Kept _____

Dates From-To _____

Name of School _____

Address _____

_____

Grade Completed or Degree _____

Remarks* _____

_____

Where Diploma Kept _____

*Outstanding activities, honors, or awards.

Dates   From-To _____

Name of School _____

Address _____

_____

Grade Completed or Degree_____

Remarks*_____

_____

Where Diploma Kept _____

Dates   From-To _____

Name of School _____

Address _____

_____

Grade Completed or Degree_____

Remarks*_____

_____

Where Diploma Kept _____

*Outstanding activities, honors, or awards.

Dates From- To _____

Name of School _____

Address _____

_____

Grade Completed or Degree _____

Remarks* _____

_____

Where Diploma Kept _____

Dates From- To _____

Name of School _____

Address _____

_____

Grade Completed or Degree _____

Remarks* _____

_____

Where Diploma Kept _____

*Outstanding activities, honors, or awards.

Military Service

SELECTIVE SERVICE

Local Board Number_____

Address _____

_____

Selective Service Number _____

Classification _____ Date _____

Reclassification_____ Date _____

Reclassification_____ Date _____

Reclassification_____ Date _____

Records Located at _____

_____

MILITARY SERVICE

Branch _____

Enlistment Date_____ Commission Date _____

Military Service Number_____

(BPED) Basic Pay Entry Date _____

(MOS) Military Occupational Status_____

Release from Active Duty _____

Rank at Discharge _____ Type _____ Date _____

Location of DD214 _____

Government Life Insurance Policy Number _____

Amount _____ Type _____

VA Certificate of Eligibility _____

VA Claim Number _____

Disability Percentage: Date_____ Disposition _____

Date _____ Disposition _____

Date _____ Disposition _____

Date _____ Disposition _____

Date _____ Disposition _____

VA Insurance Policy Number_____

Amount _____ Type _____

Other Information_____

_____

_____

Military Decorations_____

_____

_____

_____

Social Security and Employment

SOCIAL SECURITY DATA

Social Security Number _____ Date Acquired _____

Location of Card _____

Remarks _____

_____

_____

_____

EMPLOYMENT

Date From-To _____

Employer _____

Address _____

Type of Business _____

Job Title _____

Union Name, if any _____

Immediate Supervisor _____

Salary Beginning _____ Leaving _____

Benefits _____

Reason for Leaving _____

Date From-To _____

Employer _____

Address _____

Type of Business _____

Job Title _____

Union Name, if any _____

Immediate Supervisor_____

Salary Beginning _____ Leaving _____

Benefits _____

Reason for Leaving_____

Date From-To _____

Employer _____

Address _____

Type of Business _____

Job Title _____

Union Name, if any _____

Immediate Supervisor_____

Salary Beginning _____ Leaving _____

Benefits _____

Reason for Leaving_____

Date From-To _____

Employer _____

Address _____

Type of Business _____

Job Title _____

Union Name, if any _____

Immediate Supervisor _____

Salary Beginning _____ Leaving _____

Benefits _____

Reason for Leaving _____

Date From-To _____

Employer _____

Address _____

Type of Business _____

Job Title _____

Union Name, if any _____

Immediate Supervisor _____

Salary Beginning _____ Leaving _____

Benefits _____

Reason for Leaving _____

Date From-To _____

Employer _____

Address _____

Type of Business _____

Job Title _____

Union Name, if any _____

Immediate Supervisor _____

Salary Beginning _____ Leaving _____

Benefits _____

Reason for Leaving _____

Date From-To _____

Employer _____

Address _____

Type of Business _____

Job Title _____

Union Name, if any _____

Immediate Supervisor _____

Salary Beginning _____ Leaving _____

Benefits _____

Reason for Leaving _____

SELF EMPLOYMENT

Description of Business _____

_____

_____

Address _____

_____

Dates   From-To _____

Description of Business _____

_____

_____

Address _____

_____

Dates   From-To _____

Description of Business _____

_____

_____

Address _____

_____

Dates   From-To _____

UNION MEMBERSHIP

Name of Union _____

_____

Local Number_____ Membership Number_____

Dates of Membership From-To _____

Membership Fee and Dues_____

_____

Benefits _____

_____

Reasons for Leaving _____

_____

Name of Union _____

_____

Local Number_____ Membership Number_____

Dates of Membership From-To _____

Membership Fee and Dues_____

_____

Benefits _____

_____

Reasons for Leaving _____

_____

WORKMEN'S COMPENSATION

Date of Injury _____

Nature of Injury _____

Date Reported _____ Date of Award _____

Insurance Company _____

_____

Amount of Award _____

Remarks _____

_____

_____

_____

Date of Injury _____

Nature of Injury _____

Date Reported _____ Date of Award _____

Insurance Company _____

_____

Amount of Award _____

Remarks _____

_____

_____

_____

Date of Injury _____

Nature of Injury _____

Date Reported _____ Date of Award _____

Insurance Company _____

_____

Amount of Award _____

Remarks _____

_____

_____

_____

Date of Injury _____

Nature of Injury _____

Date Reported _____ Date of Award _____

Insurance Company _____

_____

Amount of Award _____

Remarks _____

_____

_____

_____

UNEMPLOYMENT COMPENSATION

Date of Registration _____ Reporting Date_____

Period of Eligibility _____

Amount Received _____

Remarks_____

_____

_____

Date of Registration _____ Reporting Date_____

Period of Eligibility _____

Amount Received _____

Remarks_____

_____

_____

Date of Registration _____ Reporting Date _____

Period of Eligibility _____

Amount Received _____

Remarks_____

_____

_____

Date of Registration _____ Reporting Date_____

Period of Eligibility _____

Amount Received _____

Remarks_____

_____

_____

Date of Registration _____ Reporting Date_____

Period of Eligibility _____

Amount Received _____

Remarks_____

_____

_____

Date of Registration _____ Reporting Date_____

Period of Eligibility _____

Amount Received _____

Remarks_____

_____

_____

Marriage

Spouse _____
             FIRST   MIDDLE   LAST

Place _____
             CITY   STATE

Date _____

Official Presiding _____

Witnesses _____

_____

Marriage License Filed at _____

Marriage Certificate Located at _____

Remarks _____

Spouse _____
             FIRST   MIDDLE   LAST

Place _____
             CITY   STATE

Date _____

Official Presiding _____

Witnesses _____

_____

Marriage License Filed at _____

Marriage Certificate Located at _____

Remarks _____

CHILDREN

Name of Child _____

Date of Birth _____ Time of Birth _____

Place of Birth _____

Where Birth Certificate Kept _____

Where Birth Certificate Registered _____

Name of Child _____

Date of Birth _____ Time of Birth _____

Place of Birth _____

Where Birth Certificate Kept _____

Where Birth Certificate Registered _____

Name of Child _____

Date of Birth _____ Time of Birth _____

Place of Birth _____

Where Birth Certificate Kept _____

Where Birth Certificate Registered _____

Name of Child _____

Date of Birth _____ Time of Birth _____

Place of Birth _____

Where Birth Certificate Kept _____

Where Birth Certificate Registered _____

Name of Child _____

Date of Birth _____ Time of Birth _____

Place of Birth _____

Where Birth Certificate Kept _____

Where Birth Certificate Registered _____

Name of Child _____

Date of Birth _____ Time of Birth _____

Place of Birth _____

Where Birth Certificate Kept _____

Where Birth Certificate Registered _____

Termination of Marriage

ANNULMENT

Effective Date _____

Attorneys _____

_____

Records Held at _____

_____

Disposition _____

_____

_____

Remarks _____

_____

SEPARATION

Effective Date _____

Attorneys _____

Records Held at _____

_____

Remarks _____

_____

DIVORCE

Effective Date _____

Attorneys _____

_____

Records Held at _____

_____

Disposition _____

_____

_____

Remarks _____

_____

Effective Date _____

Attorneys _____

_____

Records Held at _____

_____

Disposition _____

_____

_____

Remarks _____

_____

Driver's Training and License

Driver's Training School _____

Date Completed _____

Operator's License Examination   Date _____

                                         Place _____

Operator's License Number	State	Restrictions or Limitations	Renewal Date

MOTOR VEHICLE OFFENSES AND ACCIDENTS

Date	Place	Description and Disposition

MOTOR VEHICLE OFFENSES AND ACCIDENTS

Date	Place	Description and Disposition

Other Licenses

Purpose _____ Number _____

Issued by _____

Expiration Date _____

Purpose _____ Number _____

Issued by _____

Expiration Date _____

Purpose _____ Number _____

Issued by _____

Expiration Date _____

Purpose _____ Number _____

Issued by _____

Expiration Date _____

Purpose _____ Number _____

Issued by _____

Expiration Date _____

Purpose _____ Number _____

Issued by _____

Expiration Date _____

Purpose _____ Number _____

Issued by_____

Expiration Date _____

Purpose _____ Number _____

Issued by_____

Expiration Date _____

Purpose _____ Number _____

Issued by_____

Expiration Date _____

Purpose _____ Number _____

Issued by_____

Expiration Date _____

Purpose _____ Number _____

Issued by_____

Expiration Date _____

Purpose _____ Number _____

Issued by_____

Expiration Date _____

Passport

If you reside abroad for a prolonged period, you should record your passport number.

Passport Number_____

Date Issued_____ Expiration Date _____

Where Kept_____

Foreign Address _____

_____

Passport Number_____

Date Issued_____ Expiration Date _____

Where Kept_____

Foreign Address _____

_____

Passport Number_____

Date Issued_____ Expiration Date _____

Where Kept_____

Foreign Address _____

_____

Membership in Organizations

Record all social, fraternal, and professional groups to which you belong.

Name _____

Address _____

Dates   From- To_____

Offices, Honors, Awards_____

Name _____

Address _____

Dates   From-To_____

Offices, Honors, Awards_____

Name _____

Address _____

Dates   From-To_____

Offices, Honors, Awards_____

Name _____

Address _____

Dates   From-To_____

Offices, Honors, Awards_____

Name _____

Address _____

Dates   From-To _____

Offices, Honors, Awards_____

Name _____

Address _____

Dates   From-To _____

Offices, Honors, Awards_____

Name _____

Address _____

Dates   From-To _____

Offices, Honors, Awards_____

Name _____

Address _____

Dates   From-To _____

Offices, Honors, Awards_____

Publications

Title _____

Publisher _____

Address _____

Date of Publication _____

Remarks _____

_____

Title _____

Publisher _____

Address _____

Date of Publication _____

Remarks _____

_____

Title _____

Publisher _____

Address _____

Date of Publication _____

Remarks _____

_____

Title _____

Publisher _____

Address _____

Date of Publication _____

Remarks _____

_____

Title _____

Publisher _____

Address _____

Date of Publication _____

Remarks _____

_____

Title _____

Publisher _____

Address _____

Date of Publication _____

Remarks _____

_____

Elected or Appointed Governmental and Political Positions

Position Held _____

Dates   From-To _____

Duties _____

_____

Remarks _____

Position Held _____

Dates   From-To _____

Duties _____

_____

Remarks _____

Position Held _____

Dates   From-To _____

Duties _____

_____

Remarks _____

Position Held _____

Dates   From-To_____

Duties_____

_____

Remarks_____

_____

Position Held _____

Dates   From-To_____

Duties_____

_____

Remarks_____

_____

Position Held _____

Dates   From-To_____

Duties_____

_____

Remarks_____

_____

Awards and Honors

Award Received

Date _____ Place _____

Presented by _____

Remarks _____

_____

Award Received

Date _____ Place _____

Presented by _____

Remarks _____

_____

Award Received

Date _____ Place _____

Presented by _____

Remarks _____

_____

Award Received _____

Date _____ Place _____

Presented by _____

Remarks _____

_____

Award Received _____

Date _____ Place _____

Presented by _____

Remarks _____

_____

Award Received _____

Date _____ Place _____

Presented by _____

Remarks _____

_____

Award Received _____

Date _____ Place _____

Presented by _____

Remarks _____

_____

Voting Records

Date From-To _____ Place _____

Party Affiliation _____

Date From-To _____ Place _____

Party Affiliation _____

Date From-To _____ Place _____

Party Affiliation _____

Date From-To _____ Place _____

Party Affiliation _____

Date From-To _____ Place _____

Party Affiliation _____

Date From-To _____ Place _____

Party Affiliation _____

VOTES CAST

Date	Race	Vote Cast

Date	Race	Vote Cast

Date	Race	Vote Cast

Date	Race	Vote Cast

Additional Personal Records

Additional Personal Records

PART III

Medical and Dental Records

Introduction

AN adequate record of past health-related events is the foundation upon which effective health care is built. This is especially important in preventive health maintenance and also facilitates the management of acute illness.

A chronological lifetime record such as that outlined in the following pages will be appreciated by any physician who is asked to be the coordinator of your or your child's health care. A periodic, usually annual, health evaluation with appropriate entry of date is advised. This organized attention to adequate health care is typically rewarded by improved mental and physical health.

HERBERT A. HOLDEN, M.D.
Past President, American Academy of Family Physicians

Emergency Care Consent Form

The information on this page is the type of information used to give permission to a specific hospital or doctor for treatment of your child or yourself in case of an emergency. This is a suggested form for you to copy and leave available to the person responsible for the individual in the absence of the parents or guardian.

ADULT CONSENT FORM

Permission is hereby granted for the performance of any medical and surgical procedures and treatments, transfusions, diagnostic examinations, the administration of anesthetics or drugs which are deemed advisable to save my life by a licensed physician or hospital (unless otherwise stated) to or upon me.

_____

Signature and Date

Emergency Care Consent Form Location/Date_____

_____

MINOR OR WARD CONSENT FORM

Permission is hereby granted for the performance of any medical and surgical procedures and treatments, transfusions, diagnostic examinations, the administration of anesthetics or drugs which are deemed advisable to save the life of the child by a licensed physician or hospital (unless otherwise stated) to or upon_____

Name

_____

Parent or Legal Guardian and Date

Extra Space for Instructions:_____

_____

Minor or Ward Consent Form Location/Date _____

_____

Many hospitals and doctors have specific forms of their own for this purpose. They may be worded a little differently.

PERSON TO BE NOTIFIED IN CASE OF EMERGENCY

Date _____

Name _____ Relationship to Person _____

Address _____

Telephone Number _____

Date _____

Name _____ Relationship to Person _____

Address _____

Telephone Number _____

Date _____

Name _____ Relationship to Person _____

Address _____

Telephone Number _____

Date _____

Name _____ Relationship to Person _____

Address _____

Telephone Number _____

Date _____

Name _____ Relationship to Person _____

Address _____

Telephone Number _____

PERSONAL PHYSICIAN(S)

Date _____

Name _____

Address _____

Telephone Number _____

Date _____

Name _____

Address _____

Telephone Number _____

Date _____

Name _____

Address _____

Telephone Number _____

Date _____

Name _____

Address _____

Telephone Number _____

Date _____

Name _____

Address _____

Telephone Number _____

Date _____

Name _____

Address _____

Telephone Number _____

Date _____

Name _____

Address _____

Telephone Number _____

Date _____

Name _____

Address _____

Telephone Number _____

ADULT GENERAL HEALTH

Sensitivities and Allergies

Some people are allergic or oversensitive to certain substances that appear seasonally. These reactions should be recorded and discussed with the doctor. It is suggested that you wear an alerting symbol so this allergy is noted in an emergency.

Sensitive/Allergic to _____

Date(s) Diagnosed _____

Doctor _____

Test(s) Done _____

Reactions and Treatments _____

_____

_____

Sensitive/Allergic to _____

Date(s) Diagnosed _____

Doctor _____

Test(s) Done _____

Reactions and Treatments _____

_____

_____

Sensitive/Allergic to _____

Date(s) Diagnosed_____

Doctor_____

Test(s) Done _____

Reactions and Treatments _____

_____

Sensitive/Allergic to _____

Date(s) Diagnosed_____

Doctor_____

Test(s) Done _____

Reactions and Treatments _____

_____

Sensitive/Allergic to _____

Date(s) Diagnosed_____

Doctor_____

Test(s) Done _____

Reactions and Treatments _____

_____

Adult Weight Record

Date	Weight	Date	Weight

Date	Weight	Date	Weight
_____	_____	_____	_____
_____	_____	_____	_____
_____	_____	_____	_____
_____	_____	_____	_____
_____	_____	_____	_____
_____	_____	_____	_____
_____	_____	_____	_____
_____	_____	_____	_____
_____	_____	_____	_____
_____	_____	_____	_____
_____	_____	_____	_____
_____	_____	_____	_____
_____	_____	_____	_____
_____	_____	_____	_____
_____	_____	_____	_____
_____	_____	_____	_____
_____	_____	_____	_____
_____	_____	_____	_____
_____	_____	_____	_____
_____	_____	_____	_____

Physical Examinations

SCHEDULED VISITS

Date _____

Doctor or Clinic
and Address _____

_____

Height _____ Weight _____

Temperature _____ Pulse _____ Respiration _____

Blood Pressure _____ Heartbeat _____

Remarks _____

_____

Date _____

Doctor or Clinic
and Address _____

_____

Height _____ Weight _____

Temperature _____ Pulse _____ Respiration _____

Blood Pressure _____ Heartbeat _____

Remarks _____

_____

Date _____

Doctor or Clinic
and Address _____

_____

Height _____ Weight _____

Temperature _____ Pulse _____ Respiration _____

Blood Pressure _____ Heartbeat _____

Remarks _____

_____

_____

Date _____

Doctor or Clinic
and Address _____

_____

Height _____ Weight _____

Temperature _____ Pulse _____ Respiration _____

Blood Pressure _____ Heartbeat _____

Remarks _____

_____

_____

Date _____

Doctor or Clinic
and Address _____

_____

Height _____ Weight _____

Temperature _____ Pulse _____ Respiration _____

Blood Pressure _____ Heartbeat _____

Remarks _____

_____

_____

Date _____

Doctor or Clinic
and Address _____

_____

Height _____ Weight _____

Temperature _____ Pulse _____ Respiration _____

Blood Pressure _____ Heartbeat _____

Remarks _____

_____

_____

Date _____

Doctor or Clinic
and Address _____

_____

Height _____ Weight _____

Temperature _____ Pulse _____ Respiration _____

Blood Pressure _____ Heartbeat _____

Remarks _____

_____

_____

Date _____

Doctor or Clinic
and Address _____

_____

Height _____ Weight _____

Temperature _____ Pulse _____ Respiration _____

Blood Pressure _____ Heartbeat _____

Remarks _____

_____

_____

Laboratory Examinations

Date _____ Referring Physician _____

Laboratory _____

Address _____

Type of Test(s) _____

Results _____

Date _____ Referring Physician _____

Laboratory _____

Address _____

Type of Test(s) _____

Results _____

Date _____ Referring Physician _____

Laboratory _____

Address _____

Type of Test(s) _____

Results _____

Date _____ Referring Physician_____

Laboratory_____

Address_____

Type of Test(s) _____

Results _____

_____

Date _____ Referring Physician_____

Laboratory_____

Address_____

Type of Test(s) _____

Results _____

_____

Date _____ Referring Physician_____

Laboratory_____

Address_____

Type of Test(s) _____

Results _____

_____

Date _____ Referring Physician _____

Laboratory _____

Address _____

Type of Test(s) _____

Results _____

_____

Date _____ Referring Physician _____

Laboratory _____

Address _____

Type of Test(s) _____

Results _____

_____

Date _____ Referring Physician _____

Laboratory _____

Address _____

Type of Test(s) _____

Results _____

_____

X-Rays

Date_____ Referring Physician_____

Hospital or Clinic _____

Address _____

Type of X-ray _____

Remarks _____

Date_____ Referring Physician_____

Hospital or Clinic _____

Address _____

Type of X-ray _____

Remarks _____

Date_____ Referring Physician_____

Hospital or Clinic _____

Address _____

Type of X-ray _____

Remarks _____

Date_____ Referring Physician_____

Hospital or Clinic_____

Address _____

Type of X-ray _____

Remarks_____

_____

Date_____ Referring Physician_____

Hospital or Clinic_____

Address _____

Type of X-ray _____

Remarks_____

_____

Date_____ Referring Physician_____

Hospital or Clinic_____

Address _____

Type of X-ray _____

Remarks_____

_____

Date_____ Referring Physician_____

Hospital or Clinic_____

Address _____

Type of X-ray _____

Remarks_____

_____

Date_____ Referring Physician_____

Hospital or Clinic_____

Address _____

Type of X-ray _____

Remarks_____

_____

Date_____ Referring Physician_____

Hospital or Clinic_____

Address _____

Type of X-ray _____

Remarks_____

_____

Electrocardiogram

Date _____ Referring Physician _____

Hospital or Clinic _____

Address _____

Results _____

_____

Date _____ Referring Physician _____

Hospital or Clinic _____

Address _____

Results _____

_____

Date _____ Referring Physician _____

Hospital or Clinic _____

Address _____

Results _____

_____

Date _____ Referring Physician_____

Hospital or Clinic _____

Address _____

Results _____

_____

_____

Date _____ Referring Physician_____

Hospital or Clinic _____

Address _____

Results _____

_____

_____

Date _____ Referring Physician_____

Hospital or Clinic _____

Address _____

Results _____

_____

_____

Hospital Admissions

Admission Date _____

Reason(s) _____

_____

Doctor(s) _____

_____

Hospital _____

_____

Treatment _____

_____

_____

Costs _____

_____

Insurance Coverage _____

_____

Discharge Date _____

Admission Date _____

Reason(s) _____

_____

Doctor(s) _____

_____

Hospital _____

_____

Treatment _____

_____

_____

Costs _____

_____

Insurance Coverage _____

_____

Discharge Date _____

Admission Date _____

Reason(s) _____

_____

Doctor(s) _____

_____

Hospital _____

_____

Treatment _____

_____

_____

Costs_____

_____

Insurance Coverage_____

_____

Discharge Date_____

_____

Admission Date_____

Reason(s) _____

_____

Doctor(s) _____

_____

Hospital_____

_____

Treatment _____

_____

Costs_____

_____

Insurance Coverage_____

_____

Discharge Date_____

Admission Date_____

Reason(s)_____

_____

Doctor(s) _____

_____

Hospital_____

_____

Treatment _____

_____

_____

Costs_____

_____

Insurance Coverage_____

_____

Discharge Date_____

Acute Illnesses

UNSCHEDULED VISITS TO A PHYSICIAN

Illnesses having a rapid onset, *severe symptoms* and running a short course, other than contagious diseases, those requiring hospitalization, or injury.

Illness _____

Onset Date _____ Duration _____

Doctor and Address _____

_____

Treatment _____

_____

_____

Illness _____

Onset Date _____ Duration _____

Doctor and Address _____

_____

Treatment _____

_____

_____

Illness _____

Onset Date_____ Duration _____

Doctor and Address _____

_____

Treatment _____

_____

Illness _____

Onset Date_____ Duration _____

Doctor and Address _____

_____

Treatment _____

_____

Illness _____

Onset Date_____ Duration _____

Doctor and Address _____

_____

Treatment _____

_____

Accidents

Date _____ Injury _____

Place of Accident_____

Doctor_____

Place Where Treated_____

Treatment and Remarks_____
_____

Date _____ Injury _____

Place of Accident_____

Doctor_____

Place Where Treated_____

Treatment and Remarks_____
_____

Date _____ Injury _____

Place of Accident_____

Doctor_____

Place Where Treated_____

Treatment and Remarks_____
_____

Date _____ Injury _____

Place of Accident_____

Doctor_____

Place Where Treated_____

Treatment and Remarks_____

_____

Date _____ Injury _____

Place of Accident_____

Doctor_____

Place Where Treated_____

Treatment and Remarks_____

_____

Date _____ Injury _____

Place of Accident_____

Doctor_____

Place Where Treated_____

Treatment and Remarks_____

_____

Hearing and Speech Tests

HEARING

Date _____ Physician_____

Test(s) Administered _____

_____

Results and Treatment _____

_____

Date _____ Physician_____

Test(s) Administered _____

_____

Results and Treatment _____

_____

SPEECH

Date _____ Physician_____

Test(s) Administered _____

_____

Results and Treatment _____

_____

Date _____ Physician_____

Test(s) Administered _____

_____

Results and Treatment _____

_____

_____

Orthopedics

Date _____ Physician_____

Examination(s) _____

X-Rays and Other Tests_____

_____

Results _____

_____

Therapy _____

_____

_____

Date _____ Physician_____

Examination(s)_____

X-Rays and Other Tests_____

_____

Results _____

_____

Therapy _____

_____

_____

Date _____ Physician_____

Examination(s)_____

X-Rays and Other Tests_____

_____

Results _____

_____

Therapy _____

_____

_____

Chronic (Long Term) Illnesses

Illness _____ Onset Date _____

Doctor and Address _____

_____

Treatment(s) _____

_____

Illness _____ Onset Date _____

Doctor and Address _____

_____

Treatment(s) _____

_____

Illness _____ Onset Date _____

Doctor and Address _____

_____

Treatment(s) _____

_____

Illness _____ Onset Date _____

Doctor and Address _____

_____

Treatment(s) _____

_____

_____

Illness _____ Onset Date _____

Doctor and Address _____

_____

Treatment(s) _____

_____

_____

Illness _____ Onset Date _____

Doctor and Address _____

_____

Treatment(s) _____

_____

_____

Gynecology and Obstetrics

MENSTRUAL HISTORY

Date of Onset of Menstruation _____ Age _____

Number of Days Between Periods_____

Number of Days Duration _____

Changes in Menstrual Cycle _____

_____

_____

_____

_____

_____

_____

_____

_____

_____

_____

_____

Approximate Date of Termination of Menstruation_____ Age_____

CONTRACEPTIVES

Product Used _____ Date   From-To _____

Doctor or Clinic
and Address _____

_____

Remarks _____

_____

Product Used _____ Date   From-To _____

Doctor or Clinic
and Address _____

_____

Remarks _____

_____

Product Used _____ Date   From-To _____

Doctor or Clinic
and Address _____

_____

Remarks _____

_____

PAP SMEARS

Date _____ Doctor or Clinic _____

Results _____

Date _____ Doctor or Clinic _____

Results _____

Date _____ Doctor or Clinic _____

Results _____

Date _____ Doctor or Clinic _____

Results _____

Date _____ Doctor or Clinic _____

Results _____

Date _____ Doctor or Clinic _____

Results _____

Date _____ Doctor or Clinic _____

Results _____

Date _____ Doctor or Clinic _____

Results _____

Date _____ Doctor or Clinic _____

Results _____

Date _____ Doctor or Clinic_____

Results _____

Date _____ Doctor or Clinic_____

Results _____

Date _____ Doctor or Clinic_____

Results _____

Date _____ Doctor or Clinic_____

Results _____

Date _____ Doctor or Clinic_____

Results _____

Date _____ Doctor or Clinic_____

Results _____

Date _____ Doctor or Clinic_____

Results _____

Date _____ Doctor or Clinic_____

Results _____

Date _____ Doctor or Clinic_____

Results _____

Pregnancy Records

Date Confirmed _____ Weeks into Pregnancy _____

Tentative Delivery Date _____

Name and Address of Obstetrician _____

_____

Recommended Diet _____

_____

Medications Taken _____

_____

Exposure to X-Rays _____

Accidents _____

_____

Exposure to Contagious Diseases _____

_____

Hospital _____

Dates of Hospital Stay From-To _____

Date and Time of Delivery _____

History of Labor and Delivery _____

_____

_____

Date Confirmed _____ Weeks into Pregnancy _____

Tentative Delivery Date_____

Name and Addresss of Obstetrician_____

_____

Recommended Diet_____

_____

Medications Taken _____

_____

Exposure to X-Rays_____

Accidents_____

_____

Exposure to Contagious Diseases _____

_____

Hospital_____

Dates of Hospital Stay From-To_____

Date and Time of Delivery _____

History of Labor and Delivery_____

_____

_____

_____

_____

Date Confirmed _____ Weeks into Pregnancy _____

Tentative Delivery Date _____

Name and Address of Obstetrician _____

_____

Recommended Diet _____

_____

Medications Taken _____

_____

Exposure to X-Rays _____

Accidents _____

_____

Exposure to Contagious Diseases _____

_____

Hospital _____

Dates of Hospital Stay From-To _____

Date and Time of Delivery _____

History of Labor and Delivery _____

_____

_____

_____

_____

Date Confirmed _____ Weeks into Pregnancy _____

Tentative Delivery Date_____

Name and Address of Obstetrician _____

_____

Recommended Diet_____

_____

Medications Taken _____

_____

Exposure to X-Rays_____

Accidents_____

_____

Exposure to Contagious Diseases _____

_____

Hospital_____

Dates of Hospital Stay From-To_____

Date and Time of Delivery _____

History of Labor and Delivery_____

_____

_____

_____

_____

Date Confirmed _____ Weeks into Pregnancy _____

Tentative Delivery Date _____

Name and Address of Obstetrician _____

_____

Recommended Diet _____

_____

Medications Taken _____

_____

Exposure to X-Rays _____

Accidents _____

_____

Exposure to Contagious Diseases _____

_____

Hospital _____

Dates of Hospital Stay From-To _____

Date and Time of Delivery _____

History of Labor and Delivery _____

_____

_____

_____

_____

Date Confirmed _____ Weeks into Pregnancy _____

Tentative Delivery Date _____

Name and Address of Obstetrician _____

_____

Recommended Diet _____

_____

Medications Taken _____

_____

Exposure to X-Rays _____

Accidents _____

_____

Exposure to Contagious Diseases _____

_____

Hospital _____

Dates of Hospital Stay From-To _____

Date and Time of Delivery _____

History of Labor and Delivery _____

_____

_____

_____

INCOMPLETE PREGNANCIES

Your reproductive history includes spontaneous or induced abortions, miscarriages and stillbirths. If you are Rh-negative and the fetus was Rh-positive, record whether or not you were given the Rh vaccine.

Date of Termination_____ Duration _____

Circumstances _____

_____

Doctor and Address _____

_____

Date of Termination_____ Duration _____

Circumstances _____

_____

Doctor and Address _____

_____

Date of Termination_____ Duration _____

Circumstances _____

_____

Doctor and Address _____

_____

Prescribed Medications

Record only medicines that are taken regularly.

Name of Medicine _____

Doctor _____

Date   From-To_____ Prescription Number _____

Pharmacy _____

Reason for Taking _____

Name of Medicine _____

Doctor _____

Date   From-To_____ Prescription Number _____

Pharmacy _____

Reason for Taking _____

Name of Medicine _____

Doctor _____

Date   From-To_____ Prescription Number _____

Pharmacy _____

Reason for Taking _____

Adverse Reactions to Prescribed Medication

Some people have adverse reactions to certain medications. If you react to a drug that has been prescribed for you, record it here and discuss this with the doctors each time medications are prescribed. It is suggested that you wear an alerting symbol so this drug reaction will be noted in an emergency.

Name of Medicine _____

Doctor and Address _____

_____

Reason for Taking _____

Reaction _____

Name of Medicine _____

Doctor and Address _____

_____

Reason for Taking _____

Reaction _____

Name of Medicine _____

Doctor and Address _____

_____

Reason for Taking _____

Reaction _____

IMMUNIZATIONS AND IMMUNITY TESTS

Introduction

A great deal of scientific and technical development has taken place since Edward Jenner first immunized a patient against smallpox in the mid-1770s. Many of the illnesses which once killed children in large numbers can now be extremely effectively prevented through good immunization and vaccination practice. With the recent decline of certain illnesses, such as smallpox, in world importance, the advisability of routine immunization against these illnesses is now open to question. Immunization recommendations published by official bodies, such as the American Academy of Pediatrics and the United States Public Health Service, will certainly vary from time to time, depending on the need for individual immunizations. There is no question that every person should periodically reassess his own immunization status and consult his physician or other source of medical care for current information about the need for boosters and the advisability of administration of new vaccines. Immunization is no longer a process confined only to children; but, with the development of influenza vaccines and other similar preparations, adults should periodically reassess their need for new immunizations also.

PETER J. LEADLEY, M.D.
Past Director of Health,
State of Maine Department of Health and Welfare

Immunization Schedule

The American Academy of Pediatrics' recommended schedule for active immunization of normal infants and children is below. This constitutes a good preliminary guide as to childhood immunization practices; but these may be modified from year to year, and regular medical contact is advised to remain current.

2 months	DTP (Diphtheria and Tetanus combined with Pertusis [Whooping Cough] Vaccine)
	Polio
4 months	DTP
	Polio
6 months	DTP
1 year	Tuberculin Test
15 months	Rubeola (Old-Fashioned Measles) Vaccine
	Rubella (German Measles) Vaccine
	Mumps
1½ years	DTP
	Polio
4-6 years	DTP
	Polio
14-16 years	Combined Tetanus and Diphtheria; repeat every 10 years

Tetanus toxoid at time of injury: For clean, minor wounds, no booster dose is needed by a fully immunized child unless more than 10 years have elapsed since the last dose. For contaminated wounds, a booster dose should be given if more than 5 years have elapsed since the last dose.

The material above is extracted from the report of the Committee for the Control of Infectious Diseases from the American Academy of Pediatrics 1974 edition.

Immunity Tests

Test _____ Date _____

Doctor and Address _____

_____

Results _____

Test _____ Date _____

Doctor and Address _____

_____

Results _____

Test _____ Date _____

Doctor and Address _____

_____

Results _____

Test _____ Date _____

Doctor and Address _____

_____

Results _____

Immunizations

Your doctor will advise you of the best age to start your child's immunizations. Intervals between ''booster'' injections and other immunizations not previously administered are flexible and should be determined by your doctor. These records should be continued throughout your child's lifetime.

CHOLERA

Date_____ Material and Dose_____

Doctor or Clinic
and Address_____

_____

Reaction_____

_____

Next Booster Due _____

COMBINED DTP

Diphtheria, Tetanus (Lockjaw) and Pertussis (Whooping Cough)

Date_____ Material and Dose_____

Doctor or Clinic
and Address_____

_____

Reaction_____

_____

Next Booster Due _____

COMBINED TD

Tetanus and Diphtheria Toxoids (Adult Type)

Date_____ Material and Dose_____

Doctor or Clinic
and Address _____

_____

Reaction_____

Next Booster Due _____

INFLUENZA

Date_____ Material and Dose_____

Doctor or Clinic
and Address _____

_____

Reaction_____

MEASLES

Single (8 Day Regular)
Rubeola (Old-Fashioned Measles) Vaccine

Date_____ Material and Dose_____

Doctor or Clinic
and Address _____

_____

Reaction_____

Single (3 Day Measles)
Rubella (German Measles) Vaccine

Date_____ Material and Dose_____

Doctor or Clinic
and Address _____

_____

Reaction_____

Combined
Rubeola and Rubella Measles Vaccine

Date_____ Material and Dose_____

Doctor or Clinic
and Address _____

_____

Reaction_____

Rubeola, Mumps and Rubella Vaccine

Date_____ Material and Dose_____

Doctor or Clinic
and Address _____

_____

Reaction_____

MUMPS

Date_____ Material and Dose_____

Doctor or Clinic
and Address _____

_____

Reaction_____

_____

POLIO

Date_____ Material and Dose_____

Doctor or Clinic
and Address _____

_____

Reaction_____

_____

SMALLPOX

Date_____ Material and Dose_____

Doctor or Clinic
and Address _____

_____

Reaction_____

_____

TETANUS

(Single Dose)

Date_____ Material and Dose_____

Doctor or Clinic
and Address _____

_____

Reaction_____

TYPHOID FEVER

Date_____ Material and Dose_____

Doctor or Clinic
and Address _____

_____

Reaction_____

Next Booster Due _____

TYPHUS FEVER

Date_____ Material and Dose_____

Doctor or Clinic
and Address _____

_____

Reaction_____

Next Booster Due _____

YELLOW FEVER

Date_____ Material and Dose_____

Doctor or Clinic
and Address _____

_____

Reaction_____

EXTRA SPACE FOR IMMUNIZATION RECORDS

Date_____ Material and Dose_____

Doctor or Clinic
and Address _____

_____

Reaction_____

Next Booster Due _____

Date_____ Material and Dose_____

Doctor or Clinic
and Address _____

_____

Reaction_____

Next Booster Due _____

Date_____ Material and Dose_____

Doctor or Clinic
and Address _____

_____

Reaction_____

_____

Next Booster Due _____

Date_____ Material and Dose_____

Doctor or Clinic
and Address _____

_____

Reaction_____

_____

Next Booster Due _____

Date_____ Material and Dose_____

Doctor or Clinic
and Address _____

_____

Reaction_____

_____

Next Booster Due _____

CONTAGIOUS DISEASES

Introduction

CONTAGIOUS diseases are rare nowadays and not the scourge they used to be. However, we should be familiar with the common ones, the ways of preventing them, the periods of incubation and methods of transfer ("how caught"), and the times when they are most contagious (usually about two or three days before the obvious manifestations and three days or so after that). You should consult your doctor about an immunization schedule for your own family, keep it up-to-date, and be informed of other preventive methods that may be available after exposure. There is no infant immunity to chickenpox and whooping cough. Most babies are immune to the other contagious diseases for six months. In any health record it is important to have dates of specific diseases easily available (we tend to forget), as well as dates for immunization procedures that have been accomplished.

MERRITT B. LOW, M.D.
Associate Director, and Head,
Division of Chapters and Membership,
American Academy of Pediatrics

Contagious Disease Records

CHICKENPOX

Onset Date_____ Duration _____

Doctor and Address _____

_____

Treatment and Remarks_____

_____

HEPATITIS

Onset Date_____ Duration _____

Doctor and Address _____

_____

Treatment and Remarks_____

_____

MONONUCLEOSIS (GLANDULAR FEVER)

Onset Date_____ Duration _____

Doctor and Address _____

_____

Treatment and Remarks_____

_____

MUMPS

Onset Date_____ Duration _____

Doctor and Address _____

_____

Treatment and Remarks_____

_____

_____

POLIO

Onset Date_____ Duration _____

Doctor and Address _____

_____

Treatment and Remarks_____

_____

_____

RUBEOLA (OLD-FASHIONED MEASLES) (REGULAR MEASLES)

Onset Date_____ Duration _____

Doctor and Address _____

_____

Treatment and Remarks_____

_____

_____

RUBELLA (GERMAN MEASLES) (THREE-DAY MEASLES)

Onset Date_____ Duration _____

Doctor and Address _____

_____

Treatment and Remarks_____

_____

_____

SCARLET FEVER

Onset Date_____ Duration _____

Doctor and Address _____

_____

Treatment and Remarks_____

_____

_____

WHOOPING COUGH

Onset Date_____ Duration _____

Doctor and Address _____

_____

Treatment and Remarks_____

_____

_____

OTHER CONTAGIOUS DISEASES

Disease _____

Onset Date _____ Duration _____

Doctor and Address _____

_____

Treatment and Remarks _____

_____

Disease _____

Onset Date _____ Duration _____

Doctor and Address _____

_____

Treatment and Remarks _____

_____

Disease _____

Onset Date _____ Duration _____

Doctor and Address _____

_____

Treatment and Remarks _____

_____

EYE RECORDS

Introduction

TO have available reliable information about the prior status of a patient's eyes and vision can often be of inestimable value to the patient and to the physician. The visual system includes the eye and not only such obviously related structures as the eyelids and eye muscles, but also much of the brain. Eye diseases and injuries occur at every age.

When on examination the ophthalmologist finds vision to be impaired, it is helpful to know what the visual acuity was in the past. A record that lets the eye physician know of previous ocular disease at the first visit of a new patient may help in immediate diagnosis and treatment. More detailed information can be obtained later from the previous attending physician. And what ophthalmologist has not had the experience of a patient reporting an old injury, but not remembering which eye it was or who the doctor was? Faithful entries in this continuing record will at least close some of the gaps.

Other gaps in past medical information result from the facts never having been ascertained. Often when a child is brought to the ophthalmologist for treatment of an injury, parents first learn of the presence of a preexisting impairment. It sometimes happens that the condition is not as easy to treat as it would have been earlier in its course. It is especially important that the visual system be evaluated by a physician at birth, at three years and again before entering school. The information should be entered in the eye record. If any disease or abnormality is detected, the family physician will refer the patient to the ophthalmologist. The frequency of ophthalmological examination thereafter is something to be determined by the ophthalmologist. When the intervals between ophthalmological examination lengthen, periodic evaluation by the family physician will take on added importance. Entering the information here in the record will make a continuing summary available to the next physician, whether the family is ever more rooted, or ever so mobile.

CHARLES E. JAECKLE, M.D.
Past President,
American Association of Ophthalmology

Eye Examinations

Date _____

Doctor and Address _____

_____

Eyeglasses: Yes _____ No _____ Contact Lenses: Yes _____ No _____

Visual Acuity: With Lenses   Without Lenses   Intraocular Tension

Right Eye_____ _____ _____

Left Eye _____ _____ _____

Both Eyes_____ _____ _____

Near Sighted_____ Far Sighted _____

Test for Glaucoma: Yes _____ No _____ Results _____

Lenses Prescribed: Yes_____ No _____

Prescription Filled by_____

_____

Other Treatment and Remarks_____

_____

Date _____

Doctor and Address _____

_____

Eyeglasses: Yes _____ No_____ Contact Lenses: Yes _____ No_____

Visual Acuity: With Lenses   Without Lenses   Intraocular Tension

Right Eye_____   _____   _____

Left Eye _____   _____   _____

Both Eyes_____   _____   _____

Near Sighted_____ Far Sighted _____

Test for Glaucoma: Yes _____ No_____ Results _____

Lenses Prescribed: Yes_____ No_____

Prescription Filled by_____

_____

Other Treatment and Remarks_____

_____

Date _____

Doctor and Address _____

_____

Eyeglasses: Yes _____ No_____ Contact Lenses: Yes _____ No_____

Visual Acuity: With Lenses   Without Lenses   Intraocular Tension

Right Eye_____   _____   _____

Left Eye _____   _____   _____

Both Eyes_____   _____   _____

Near Sighted_____ Far Sighted _____

Test for Glaucoma: Yes _____ No _____ Results _____

Lenses Prescribed: Yes _____ No _____

Prescription Filled by_____

_____

Other Treatment and Remarks_____

_____

Date _____

Doctor and Address _____

_____

Eyeglasses: Yes _____ No _____ Contact Lenses: Yes _____ No _____

Visual Acuity: With Lenses   Without Lenses   Intraocular Tension

Right Eye_____   _____   _____

Left Eye _____   _____   _____

Both Eyes_____   _____   _____

Near Sighted_____ Far Sighted _____

Test for Glaucoma: Yes _____ No _____ Results _____

Lenses Prescribed: Yes _____ No _____

Prescription Filled by_____

_____

Other Treatment and Remarks_____

_____

Date _____

Doctor and Address _____

_____

Eyeglasses: Yes _____ No_____ Contact Lenses: Yes _____ No_____

Visual Acuity: With Lenses   Without Lenses   Intraocular Tension

Right Eye_____   _____   _____

Left Eye _____   _____   _____

Both Eyes_____   _____   _____

Near Sighted_____ Far Sighted _____

Test for Glaucoma: Yes _____ No_____ Results _____

Lenses Prescribed: Yes_____ No _____

Prescription Filled by_____

_____

Other Treatment and Remarks_____

_____

Date _____

Doctor and Address _____

Eyeglasses: Yes _____ No _____ Contact Lenses: Yes _____ No _____

Visual Acuity: With Lenses   Without Lenses   Intraocular Tension

Right Eye_____   _____   _____

Left Eye _____   _____   _____

Both Eyes_____   _____   _____

Near Sighted_____ Far Sighted _____

Test for Glaucoma: Yes _____ No_____ Results _____

Lenses Prescribed: Yes_____ No _____

Prescription Filled by_____

_____

Other Treatment and Remarks_____

_____

Date _____

Doctor and Address _____

_____

Eyeglasses: Yes _____ No _____ Contact Lenses: Yes _____ No _____

Visual Acuity: With Lenses   Without Lenses   Intraocular Tension

Right Eye_____   _____   _____

Left Eye _____   _____   _____

Both Eyes_____   _____   _____

Near Sighted _____ Far Sighted _____

Test for Glaucoma: Yes _____ No _____ Results _____

Lenses Prescribed: Yes _____ No _____

Prescription Filled by _____

_____

Other Treatment and Remarks _____

Date _____

Doctor and Address _____

_____

Eyeglasses: Yes _____ No _____   Contact Lenses: Yes _____ No _____

Visual Acuity: With Lenses   Without Lenses   Intraocular Tension

Right Eye _____   _____   _____

Left Eye _____   _____   _____

Both Eyes _____   _____   _____

Near Sighted _____ Far Sighted _____

Test for Glaucoma: Yes _____ No _____ Results _____

Lenses Prescribed: Yes _____ No _____

Prescription Filled by _____

_____

Other Treatment and Remarks _____

PSYCHIATRIC HISTORY

Psychiatric Records

Psychiatrist _____

Address _____

Seen From-To _____ Sessions Per Week _____

Treatment and Results _____

_____

Psychiatrist _____

Address _____

Seen From-To _____ Sessions Per Week _____

Treatment and Results _____

_____

Psychiatrist _____

Address _____

Seen From-To _____ Sessions Per Week _____

Treatment and Results _____

_____

Psychiatrist _____

Address _____

Seen   From-To _____ Sessions Per Week _____

Treatment and Results _____

_____

_____

Psychiatrist _____

Address _____

Seen   From-To _____ Sessions Per Week _____

Treatment and Results _____

_____

_____

Psychiatrist _____

Address _____

Seen   From-To _____ Sessions Per Week _____

Treatment and Results _____

_____

_____

ADULT DENTAL RECORDS

Introduction

DENTAL health is a matter of lifelong concern. Persons of all ages can and should have a healthy mouth and a pleasant smile. With proper personal and professional care, a person can keep his permanent teeth all his life, as nature intended. Healthy, well-cared-for teeth are importan for chewing food properly, for normal speech, and for an attractive appearance.

Good oral health is the result of three factors:

(1) Proper home care—Parents should start brushing a child's teeth after the first incisors (front teeth) have erupted. By the time the child has all of his primary teeth, he will be used to the idea and can begin to learn to brush his teeth himself. Daily brushing and flossing are important to remove debris and plaque and thereby help prevent dental caries and gum disease.

(2) Professional care—The child should make his first visit to the dentist between two and three years of age, when all 20 of the primary teeth have erupted. In general, dental visits should continue every six months, or as often as the dentist recommends. Regular visits enable the dentist to provide dental health education and discover new cavities and other signs of disease at an early stage, when they can most easily be corrected. A record should be kept of the name and address of each dentist who provides care for the child. While it is not necessary to record the procedures performed during each dental visit, a list of appointment dates can encourage regular visits to the dentist.

(3) Balanced diet—A well-balanced, adequate and varied diet which promotes general health will also promote oral health. One food nutrient which can provide additional decay resistance is fluoride. If the community water supply is deficient in fluoride, the dentist can provide supplemental fluoride. To minimize decay it is important that a child's consumption of fermentable carbohydrates, especially sugar, be limited. Sweets are the least harmful when eaten at mealtime and the most harmful when they are used as between-meal snacks.

The future in dental health is much brighter today than ever before. Although not all dental diseases can be prevented, there is much that the dentist and the patient can do now to assure longer-lasting natural teeth and good oral health. It is far better to prevent dental disease than to repair the damage.

American Dental Association

Permanent Teeth

TOOTH NUMBER | **NAME**

TOOTH NUMBER	NAME
1	Upper right 3rd molar
2	Upper right 2nd molar
3	Upper right 1st molar
4	Upper right 2nd bicuspid or pre-molar
5	Upper right 1st bicuspid or pre-molar
6	Upper right cuspid
7	Upper right lateral incisor
8	Upper right central incisor
9	Upper left central incisor
10	Upper left lateral incisor
11	Upper left cuspid
12	Upper left 1st bicuspid or pre-molar
13	Upper left 2nd bicuspid or pre-molar
14	Upper left 1st molar
15	Upper left 2nd molar
16	Upper left 3rd molar
17	Lower left 3rd molar
18	Lower left 2nd molar
19	Lower left 1st molar
20	Lower left 2nd bicuspid or pre-molar
21	Lower left 1st bicuspid or pre-molar
22	Lower left cuspid
23	Lower left lateral incisor
24	Lower left central incisor
25	Lower right central incisor
26	Lower right lateral incisor
27	Lower right cuspid
28	Lower right 1st pre-molar
29	Lower right 2nd pre-molar
30	Lower right 1st molar
31	Lower right 2nd molar
32	Lower right 3rd molar

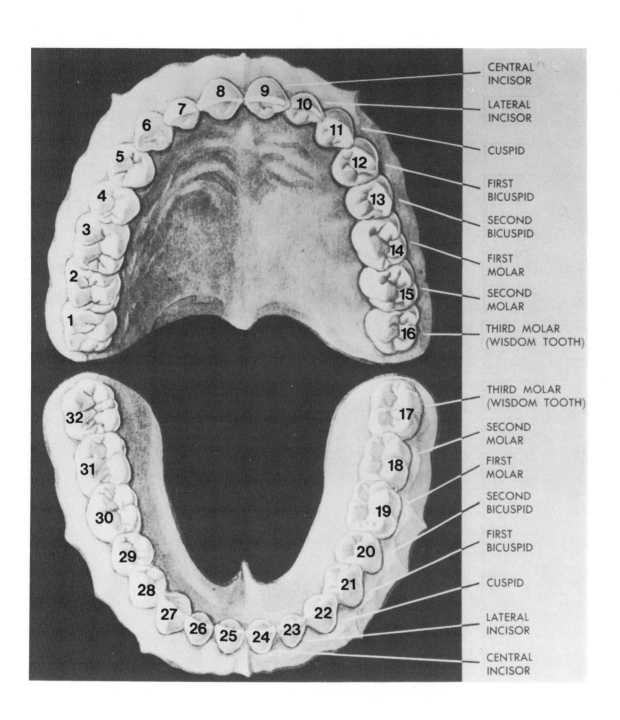

CENTRAL
INCISOR

LATERAL
INCISOR

CUSPID

FIRST
BICUSPID

SECOND
BICUSPID

FIRST
MOLAR

SECOND
MOLAR

THIRD MOLAR
(WISDOM TOOTH)

THIRD MOLAR
(WISDOM TOOTH)

SECOND
MOLAR

FIRST
MOLAR

SECOND
BICUSPID

FIRST
BICUSPID

CUSPID

LATERAL
INCISOR

CENTRAL
INCISOR

ERUPTION AND SHEDDING OF PRIMARY TEETH

Upper	Eruption	Shedding
Central incisor	8-12 mo.	6- 7 yr.
Lateral incisor	9-13 mo.	7- 8 yr.
Cuspid	16-22 mo.	10-12 yr.
First molar	13-19 mo.	9-11 yr.
Second molar	25-33 mo.	10-12 yr.
Lower		
Second molar	23-31 mo.	10-12 yr.
First molar	14-18 mo.	9-11 yr.
Cuspid	17-23 mo.	9-12 yr.
Lateral incisor	10-16 mo.	7- 8 yr.
Central incisor	6-10 mo.	6- 7 yr.

See p. 30 for above dates.

ERUPTION OF PERMANENT TEETH

	Upper	Date	Lower	Date
Central incisor	7- 8 yr.	_____	6- 7 yr.	_____
Lateral incisor	8- 9 yr.	_____	7- 8 yr.	_____
Cuspid	11-12 yr.	_____	9-10 yr.	_____
First bicuspid	10-11 yr.	_____	10-12 yr.	_____
Second bicuspid	10-12 yr.	_____	11-12 yr.	_____
First molar	6- 7 yr.	_____	6- 7 yr.	_____
Second molar	12-13 yr.	_____	11-13 yr.	_____
Third molar	17-21 yr.	_____	17-21 yr.	_____

Adult Dental Examinations

Date _____

Dentist _____

Address _____

Work Done _____

Work Needed _____

Remarks _____

_____

_____

_____

Date _____

Dentist _____

Address _____

Work Done _____

Work Needed _____

Remarks _____

_____

_____

_____

Date _____

Dentist _____

Address _____

Work Done _____

Work Needed _____

Remarks _____

_____

Date _____

Dentist _____

Address _____

Work Done _____

Work Needed _____

Remarks _____

_____

Date _____

Dentist _____

Address _____

Work Done _____

Work Needed _____

Remarks _____

_____

Date _____

Dentist _____

Address _____

Work Done _____

Work Needed _____

Remarks _____

_____

Date _____

Dentist _____

Address _____

Work Done _____

Work Needed _____

Remarks _____

_____

Date _____

Dentist _____

Address _____

Work Done _____

Work Needed _____

Remarks _____

_____

Date _____

Dentist _____

Address _____

Work Done _____

Work Needed _____

Remarks _____

_____

Date _____

Dentist _____

Address _____

Work Done _____

Work Needed _____

Remarks _____

_____

Date _____

Dentist _____

Address _____

Work Done _____

Work Needed _____

Remarks _____

_____

Additional Health Records

Additional Health Records

PART IV

Property Records

Introduction

RECORD keeping for legal purposes is essential. We need records each year to figure our income taxes. And, whenever we wish to make a gift of a substantial nature, it is essential to have an accurate record of the property's purchase price. Of course, records of all major buying and selling transactions should be kept. It is also advisable to keep records of property received through gifts or by inheritance. And, in the case of death, an accurate record of property values is essential for efficient probate of the estate.

It is definitely to your and your family's advantage to keep accurate and up-to-date property records. They will be of great help when you consult with an attorney. And, a glance over them often might indicate when you should consult with a lawyer. Of course, this always should be before you have encountered a true legal problem; a lawyer can be most helpful when his advice is sought when there is only a possibility that some legal difficulty might develop, not when a legal problem is actually full-blown. You should get in the habit of consulting with an attorney each year and reviewing your entire legal profile with him. An annual legal check-up should become part of your routine, like an annual medical check-up.

JAMES D. FELLERS, Esq.
Past President, American Bar Association

Last Will and Testament

WILL

Dated_____ Attorney's Name and Address_____

_____

Location of Original_____

Location of Copy_____

Executor's Name and Address_____

_____

Guardian's Name and Address_____

_____

Testamentary Trust Trustee's Name and Address_____

_____

If Will Destroyed, Date and Method of Destruction_____

_____

CODICILS

Dated_____ Location_____

Dated_____ Location_____

Dated_____ Location_____

Dated_____ Location_____

Dated_____ Location_____

DEED OF TRUST

Dated_____

Trustee's Name and Address_____

_____

Beneficiaries_____

_____

_____

_____

Corpus of Trust_____

Location_____

WILL

Dated_____ Attorney's Name and Address_____

_____

Location of Original_____

Location of Copy_____

Executor's Name and Address_____

_____

Guardian's Name and Address_____

_____

Testamentary Trust Trustee's Name and Address_____

_____

If Will Destroyed, Date and Method of Destruction_____

_____

CODICILS

Dated_____ Location_____

Dated_____ Location_____

Dated_____ Location_____

Dated_____ Location_____

Dated_____ Location_____

Dated_____ Location_____

DEED OF TRUST

Dated_____

Trustee's Name and Address_____

_____

Beneficiaries_____

_____

_____

_____

_____

Corpus of Trust_____

Location_____

Information in the Event of My Death

SOCIAL SECURITY

Social Security Number _____

Location of Social Security Card _____

_____

Location of Employment Record Showing Social Security Payments _____

_____

MILITARY SERVICE

I am ☐   am not ☐   a veteran of the U.S. Armed Forces.

Active Duty from _____ to _____

Branch_____ Rank _____

Service Serial Number_____

Military Papers Located _____

AVAILABILITY OF IMMEDIATE CASH

Lump Sum Insurance _____

Company(s)_____

_____

Lump Sum Social Security _____

Other Money Available_____

_____

FUNERAL ARRANGEMENTS

Religious Preference _____

I would ☐   would not ☐   like full Military Honors.

I would ☐   would not ☐   like a fraternal funeral.

Remarks _____

Funeral Director _____

Address _____ Telephone _____

Burial Information:

Cemetery _____ Address _____

I wish to be buried ☐   cremated ☐

Burial Contract Date _____ Cremation Contract Date _____

I do ☐   do not ☐   have a niche or lot.

Location _____ Lot Purchase Date _____

PERPETUAL CARE

Amount Paid $ _____ Date _____

Special Services Desired _____

_____

I would prefer flowers ☐   contributions to charity ☐

Name of Charity _____

Address _____
Request undertaker to provide _____ copies of my death certificate. (Copies will be needed by each life insurance company, for real estate title transfer, government benefits, social security and VA, personal property and securities, stocks/bonds, vehicle registrations, etc.)

ANATOMICAL BEQUEST

_____

_____

_____

PERSONS TO BE NOTIFIED IN CASE OF DEATH

Name _____ Telephone _____

Address _____

Name _____ Telephone _____

Address _____

Name _____ Telephone _____

Address _____

Additional Addresses in My Address Book, Located at _____

_____

POWER OF ATTORNEY

Name _____ General or Special _____

Location of Documents_____

Dated _____ Revoked_____

Name _____ General or Special _____

Location of Documents _____

Dated _____ Revoked_____

ESTATE PLANNERS

Attorney   Accountant

_____   _____

_____   _____

_____   _____

_____   _____

Insurance Agent   Trust Officer

_____   _____

_____   _____

_____   _____

_____   _____

Remarks_____

_____

_____

_____

_____

_____

_____

_____

_____

Reportable Gifts and Donations

Date _____ Recipient _____

Gift _____ Value _____

Date _____ Recipient _____

Gift _____ Value _____

Date _____ Recipient _____

Gift _____ Value _____

Date _____ Recipient _____

Gift _____ Value _____

Date _____ Recipient _____

Gift _____ Value _____

Date _____ Recipient _____

Gift _____ Value _____

Date _____ Recipient _____

Gift _____ Value _____

Date _____ Recipient _____

Gift _____ Value _____

Date _____ Recipient _____

Gift _____ Value _____

Date _____ Recipient _____

Gift _____ Value _____

Date _____ Recipient _____

Gift _____ Value _____

Date _____ Recipient _____

Gift _____ Value _____

Date _____ Recipient _____

Gift _____ Value _____

Date _____ Recipient _____

Gift _____ Value _____

Date _____ Recipient _____

Gift _____ Value _____

Date _____ Recipient _____

Gift _____ Value _____

Date _____ Recipient _____

Gift _____ Value _____

Date _____ Recipient _____

Gift _____ Value _____

Date _____ Recipient _____

Gift _____ Value _____

Date _____ Recipient _____

Gift _____ Value _____

Date _____ Recipient _____

Gift _____ Value _____

Date _____ Recipient _____

Gift _____ Value _____

Date _____ Recipient _____

Gift _____ Value _____

Date _____ Recipient _____

Gift _____ Value _____

Date _____ Recipient _____

Gift _____ Value _____

Date _____ Recipient _____

Gift _____ Value _____

Current Creditors

Date _____ Name _____ Amount _____

Reason _____

If Paid, Location of Discharge Papers _____

Location of Supporting Documents _____

Date _____ Name _____ Amount _____

Reason _____

If Paid, Location of Discharge Papers _____

Location of Supporting Documents _____

Date _____ Name _____ Amount _____

Reason _____

If Paid, Location of Discharge Papers _____

Location of Supporting Documents _____

Date _____ Name _____ Amount _____

Reason _____

If Paid, Location of Discharge Papers _____

Location of Supporting Documents _____

Date _____ Name _____ Amount _____

Reason _____

If Paid, Location of Discharge Papers _____

Location of Supporting Documents _____

Date _____ Name _____ Amount _____

Reason _____

If Paid, Location of Discharge Papers _____

Location of Supporting Documents _____

Date _____ Name _____ Amount _____

Reason _____

If Paid, Location of Discharge Papers _____

Location of Supporting Documents _____

Date _____ Name _____ Amount _____

Reason _____

If Paid, Location of Discharge Papers _____

Location of Supporting Documents _____

Date _____ Name _____ Amount _____

Reason _____

If Paid, Location of Discharge Papers _____

Location of Supporting Documents _____

Current Debtors

Date _____ Name _____ Amount _____

Reason _____

Security, if any_____

Location of Supporting Documents _____

Date _____ Name _____ Amount _____

Reason _____

Security, if any_____

Location of Supporting Documents _____

Date _____ Name _____ Amount _____

Reason _____

Security, if any_____

Location of Supporting Documents _____

Date _____ Name _____ Amount _____

Reason _____

Security, if any_____

Location of Supporting Documents _____

Current Net Worth

INVENTORY OF PERSONAL ASSETS

19_____   **ASSETS — WHAT I OWN**

Cash in Bank (Checking)
_____

Savings in Bank
_____

Stocks (Market Value)
_____

_____

Bonds (Market Value)
_____

_____

_____

Insurance (Cash-Surrender Value)
_____

Real Estate (Present Value)
_____

Household Goods (Present Value)
_____

Auto (Trade-In Value)
_____

Annuities/Pensions (Cash-Surrender Value)
_____

Other Assets
_____

_____

_____

TOTAL ASSETS
_____

DEDUCT TOTAL LIABILITIES
_____

NET WORTH

AND LIABILITIES

LIABILITIES — WHAT I OWE   19____

Mortgage

Loans

Interest Due

Balance Due on

Installment Purchases

Other Obligations

TOTAL LIABILITIES

INVENTORY OF PERSONAL ASSETS

19_____   **ASSETS — WHAT I OWN**

Cash in Bank (Checking)
_____

Savings in Bank
_____

Stocks (Market Value)
_____

_____

Bonds (Market Value)
_____

_____

_____

Insurance (Cash-Surrender Value)
_____

Real Estate (Present Value)
_____

Household Goods (Present Value)
_____

Auto (Trade-In Value)
_____

Annuities/Pensions (Cash-Surrender Value)
_____

Other Assets
_____

_____

_____

TOTAL ASSETS
_____

DEDUCT TOTAL LIABILITIES
_____

NET WORTH
_____

AND LIABILITIES

LIABILITIES — WHAT I OWE   19____

Mortgage
_____

Loans
_____

_____

_____

Interest Due
_____

_____

Balance Due on
_____

Installment Purchases
_____

_____

_____

_____

Other Obligations
_____

_____

_____

_____

TOTAL LIABILITIES
_____

_____

_____

INVENTORY OF PERSONAL ASSETS

19_____   **ASSETS — WHAT I OWN**

Cash in Bank (Checking)

Savings in Bank

Stocks (Market Value)

Bonds (Market Value)

Insúrance (Cash-Surrender Value)

Real Estate (Present Value)

Household Goods (Present Value)

Auto (Trade-In Value)

Annuities/Pensions (Cash-Surrender Value)

Other Assets

TOTAL ASSETS

DEDUCT TOTAL LIABILITIES

NET WORTH

AND LIABILITIES

LIABILITIES — WHAT I OWE   19____

Mortgage

Loans

Interest Due

Balance Due on

Installment Purchases

Other Obligations

TOTAL LIABILITIES

INVENTORY OF PERSONAL ASSETS

19_____   **ASSETS — WHAT I OWN**

Cash in Bank (Checking)

Savings in Bank

Stocks (Market Value)

Bonds (Market Value)

Insurance (Cash-Surrender Value)

Real Estate (Present Value)

Household Goods (Present Value)

Auto (Trade-In Value)

Annuities/Pensions (Cash-Surrender Value)

Other Assets

TOTAL ASSETS

DEDUCT TOTAL LIABILITIES

NET WORTH

AND LIABILITIES

LIABILITIES — WHAT I OWE   19____

Mortgage

Loans

Interest Due

Balance Due on

Installment Purchases

Other Obligations

TOTAL LIABILITIES

INVENTORY OF PERSONAL ASSETS

19____   **ASSETS — WHAT I OWN**

Cash in Bank (Checking)

Savings in Bank

Stocks (Market Value)

Bonds (Market Value)

Insurance (Cash-Surrender Value)

Real Estate (Present Value)

Household Goods (Present Value)

Auto (Trade-In Value)

Annuities/Pensions (Cash-Surrender Value)

Other Assets

TOTAL ASSETS

DEDUCT TOTAL LIABILITIES

NET WORTH

AND LIABILITIES

LIABILITIES — WHAT I OWE   19____

Mortgage _____

Loans _____

_____

_____

Interest Due _____

_____

Balance Due on _____

Installment Purchases _____

_____

_____

_____

Other Obligations _____

_____

_____

TOTAL LIABILITIES _____

_____

INVENTORY OF PERSONAL ASSETS

19_____   **ASSETS — WHAT I OWN**

Cash in Bank (Checking)

Savings in Bank

Stocks (Market Value)

Bonds (Market Value)

Insurance (Cash-Surrender Value)

Real Estate (Present Value)

Household Goods (Present Value)

Auto (Trade-In Value)

Annuities/Pensions (Cash-Surrender Value)

Other Assets

TOTAL ASSETS

DEDUCT TOTAL LIABILITIES

NET WORTH

AND LIABILITIES

LIABILITIES — WHAT I OWE   19____

Mortgage
_____

Loans
_____

_____

_____

Interest Due
_____

_____

Balance Due on
_____

Installment Purchases
_____

_____

_____

_____

Other Obligations
_____

_____

_____

_____

TOTAL LIABILITIES
_____

_____

_____

INVENTORY OF PERSONAL ASSETS

19_____ **ASSETS — WHAT I OWN**

Cash in Bank (Checking)

Savings in Bank

Stocks (Market Value)

Bonds (Market Value)

Insurance (Cash-Surrender Value)

Real Estate (Present Value)

Household Goods (Present Value)

Auto (Trade-In Value)

Annuities/Pensions (Cash-Surrender Value)

Other Assets

TOTAL ASSETS

DEDUCT TOTAL LIABILITIES

NET WORTH

AND LIABILITIES

LIABILITIES — WHAT I OWE   19____

Mortgage
_____

Loans
_____

_____

_____

Interest Due
_____

_____

Balance Due on
_____

Installment Purchases
_____

_____

_____

_____

Other Obligations
_____

_____

_____

_____

TOTAL LIABILITIES
_____

_____

_____

INVENTORY OF PERSONAL ASSETS

19____   **ASSETS — WHAT I OWN**

Cash in Bank (Checking)
_____

Savings in Bank
_____

Stocks (Market Value)
_____

_____

Bonds (Market Value)
_____

_____

_____

Insurance (Cash-Surrender Value)
_____

Real Estate (Present Value)
_____

Household Goods (Present Value)
_____

Auto (Trade-In Value)
_____

Annuities/Pensions (Cash-Surrender Value)
_____

Other Assets
_____

_____

_____

TOTAL ASSETS
_____

DEDUCT TOTAL LIABILITIES
_____

NET WORTH
_____

AND LIABILITIES

LIABILITIES — WHAT I OWE   19____

Mortgage _____

Loans _____

_____

_____

Interest Due _____

_____

Balance Due on _____

Installment Purchases _____

_____

_____

_____

Other Obligations _____

_____

_____

_____

TOTAL LIABILITIES _____

_____

_____

INVENTORY OF PERSONAL ASSETS

19_____   **ASSETS — WHAT I OWN**

Cash in Bank (Checking)
_____

Savings in Bank
_____

Stocks (Market Value)
_____

_____

Bonds (Market Value)
_____

_____

_____

Insurance (Cash-Surrender Value)
_____

Real Estate (Present Value)
_____

Household Goods (Present Value)
_____

Auto (Trade-In Value)
_____

Annuities/Pensions (Cash-Surrender Value)
_____

Other Assets
_____

_____

TOTAL ASSETS
_____

DEDUCT TOTAL LIABILITIES
_____

NET WORTH
_____

AND LIABILITIES

LIABILITIES — WHAT I OWE   19____

Mortgage
_____

Loans
_____

_____

_____

Interest Due
_____

_____

Balance Due on
_____

Installment Purchases
_____

_____

_____

_____

Other Obligations
_____

_____

_____

TOTAL LIABILITIES
_____

_____

_____

INVENTORY OF PERSONAL ASSETS

19_____   **ASSETS — WHAT I OWN**

Cash in Bank (Checking)

Savings in Bank

Stocks (Market Value)

Bonds (Market Value)

Insurance (Cash-Surrender Value)

Real Estate (Present Value)

Household Goods (Present Value)

Auto (Trade-In Value)

Annuities/Pensions (Cash-Surrender Value)

Other Assets

TOTAL ASSETS

DEDUCT TOTAL LIABILITIES

NET WORTH

AND LIABILITIES

LIABILITIES — WHAT I OWE   19____

Mortgage

Loans

Interest Due

Balance Due on

Installment Purchases

Other Obligations

TOTAL LIABILITIES

Stocks and Bonds

STOCKS

Date Acquired _____ Shares _____ Price _____

Corporation _____

Certificate Number _____

Broker _____

Date Sold _____ Shares _____ Price _____

Date Acquired _____ Shares _____ Price _____

Corporation _____

Certificate Number _____

Broker _____

Date Sold _____ Shares _____ Price _____

Date Acquired _____ Shares _____ Price _____

Corporation _____

Certificate Number _____

Broker _____

Date Sold _____ Shares _____ Price _____

Date Acquired _____ Shares_____ Price _____

Corporation_____

Certificate Number_____

Broker_____

Date Sold_____ Shares_____ Price _____

Date Acquired _____ Shares_____ Price _____

Corporation_____

Certificate Number_____

Broker_____

Date Sold_____ Shares_____ Price _____

Date Acquired _____ Shares_____ Price _____

Corporation_____

Certificate Number_____

Broker_____

Date Sold_____ Shares_____ Price _____

Date Acquired _____ Shares_____ Price _____

Corporation_____

Certificate Number_____

Broker_____

Date Sold_____ Shares_____ Price _____

Date Acquired _____ Shares_____ Price _____

Corporation_____

Certificate Number_____

Broker_____

Date Sold_____ Shares_____ Price _____

Date Acquired _____ Shares_____ Price _____

Corporation_____

Certificate Number_____

Broker_____

Date Sold_____ Shares_____ Price _____

Date Acquired _____ Shares_____ Price _____

Corporation_____

Certificate Number_____

Broker_____

Date Sold_____ Shares_____ Price _____

Date Acquired _____ Shares_____ Price _____

Corporation_____

Certificate Number_____

Broker_____

Date Sold_____ Shares_____ Price _____

Date Acquired _____ Shares _____ Price _____

Corporation _____

Certificate Number _____

Broker _____

Date Sold _____ Shares _____ Price _____

Date Acquired _____ Shares _____ Price _____

Corporation _____

Certificate Number _____

Broker _____

Date Sold _____ Shares _____ Price _____

Date Acquired _____ Shares _____ Price _____

Corporation _____

Certificate Number _____

Broker _____

Date Sold _____ Shares _____ Price _____

Date Acquired _____ Shares _____ Price _____

Corporation _____

Certificate Number _____

Broker _____

Date Sold _____ Shares _____ Price _____

Date Acquired _____ Shares_____ Price _____

Corporation_____

Certificate Number_____

Broker_____

Date Sold_____ Shares_____ Price _____

Date Acquired _____ Shares_____ Price _____

Corporation_____

Certificate Number_____

Broker_____

Date Sold_____ Shares_____ Price _____

Date Acquired _____ Shares_____ Price _____

Corporation_____

Certificate Number_____

Broker_____

Date Sold_____ Shares_____ Price _____

Date Acquired _____ Shares_____ Price _____

Corporation_____

Certificate Number_____

Broker_____

Date Sold_____ Shares_____ Price _____

BONDS

Date Acquired _____ Type _____ Price _____

Broker_____

Certificate Number_____ Maturity Date_____

Tax Status _____

Date Redeemed _____ Price _____

Date Acquired _____ Type _____ Price _____

Broker_____

Certificate Number_____ Maturity Date_____

Tax Status _____

Date Redeemed _____ Price _____

Date Acquired _____ Type _____ Price _____

Broker_____

Certificate Number_____ Maturity Date_____

Tax Status _____

Date Redeemed _____ Price _____

Date Acquired _____ Type _____ Price _____

Broker_____

Certificate Number_____ Maturity Date_____

Tax Status _____

Date Redeemed _____ Price _____

Date Acquired _____ Type _____ Price _____

Broker_____

Certificate Number _____ Maturity Date_____

Tax Status _____

Date Redeemed _____ Price _____

Date Acquired _____ Type _____ Price _____

Broker_____

Certificate Number _____ Maturity Date_____

Tax Status _____

Date Redeemed _____ Price _____

Date Acquired _____ Type _____ Price _____

Broker_____

Certificate Number _____ Maturity Date_____

Tax Status _____

Date Redeemed _____ Price _____

Date Acquired _____ Type _____ Price _____

Broker_____

Certificate Number _____ Maturity Date_____

Tax Status _____

Date Redeemed _____ Price _____

Trust Property

Nature of Property _____

Settlor _____

Amount/Value _____ Date _____

Beneficiary _____

Location _____

Conditions of Trust _____

_____

_____

_____

Nature of Property _____

Settlor _____

Amount/Value _____ Date _____

Beneficiary _____

Location _____

Conditions of Trust _____

_____

_____

_____

Nature of Property _____

Settlor _____

Amount/Value _____ Date _____

Beneficiary _____

Location _____

Conditions of Trust _____

_____

_____

_____

_____

Nature of Property _____

Settlor _____

Amount/Value _____ Date _____

Beneficiary _____

Location _____

Conditions of Trust _____

_____

_____

_____

_____

Other Investments

Real Estate

Location and Description _____

_____

Purchased from_____

Deed Dated_____

Recorded _____ Book _____ Page _____ County_____

In Name of _____

Purchase Price _____

IMPROVEMENTS

Description	Date	Value
_____	_____	_____
_____	_____	_____
_____	_____	_____

MORTGAGES

Date _____ Mortgage in Name of_____

Mortgage Held by_____

Attorneys_____

Location of Deed_____

Conveyed to _____ by _____

Deed Dated_____ Sales Price_____

Location and Description _____

_____

Purchased from _____

Deed Dated _____

Recorded _____ Book _____ Page _____ County _____

In Name of _____

Purchase Price _____

IMPROVEMENTS

Description	Date	Value
_____	_____	_____
_____	_____	_____
_____	_____	_____

MORTGAGES

Date _____ Mortgage in Name of _____

Mortgage Held by _____

Attorneys _____

Location of Deed _____

Conveyed to _____ by _____

Deed Dated _____ Sales Price _____

Location and Description _____

_____

Purchased from _____

Deed Dated _____

Recorded _____ Book _____ Page _____ County_____

In Name of _____

Purchase Price _____

IMPROVEMENTS

Description	Date	Value
_____	_____	_____
_____	_____	_____
_____	_____	_____
_____	_____	_____

MORTGAGES

Date _____ Mortgage in Name of_____

Mortgage Held by _____

Attorneys_____

Location of Deed _____

Conveyed to _____ by _____

Deed Dated_____ Sales Price_____

Location and Description _____

_____

Purchased from _____

Deed Dated _____

Recorded _____ Book _____ Page _____ County _____

In Name of _____

Purchase Price _____

IMPROVEMENTS

Description	Date	Value
_____	_____	_____
_____	_____	_____
_____	_____	_____
_____	_____	_____

MORTGAGES

Date _____ Mortgage in Name of _____

Mortgage Held by _____

Attorneys _____

Location of Deed _____

Conveyed to _____ by _____

Deed Dated _____ Sales Price _____

Location and Description _____

_____

Purchased from _____

Deed Dated_____

Recorded _____ Book _____ Page _____ County_____

In Name of _____

Purchase Price _____

IMPROVEMENTS

Description	Date	Value
_____	_____	_____
_____	_____	_____
_____	_____	_____
_____	_____	_____

MORTGAGES

Date _____ Mortgage in Name of_____

Mortgage Held by_____

Attorneys_____

Location of Deed_____

Conveyed to _____ by _____

Deed Dated_____ Sales Price_____

Rental Property

Address _____

Owner/Landlord _____

Date From-To _____ Rental Price _____

Address _____

Owner/Landlord _____

Date From-To _____ Rental Price _____

Address _____

Owner/Landlord _____

Date From-To _____ Rental Price _____

Address _____

Owner/Landlord _____

Date From-To _____ Rental Price _____

Address _____

Owner/Landlord _____

Date From-To _____ Rental Price _____

Address _____

Owner/Landlord _____

Date From-To _____ Rental Price _____

Address _____

Owner/Landlord _____

Date From-To _____ Rental Price _____

Address _____

Owner/Landlord _____

Date From-To _____ Rental Price _____

Address _____

Owner/Landlord _____

Date From-To _____ Rental Price _____

Address _____

Owner/Landlord _____

Date From-To _____ Rental Price _____

Address _____

Owner/Landlord _____

Date From-To _____ Rental Price _____

Motor Vehicles

Make_____ Year_____ Model_____

Purchased from _____

Date of Purchase _____ Price _____ ID/VIN Number _____

Sales/ Trade Date_____ Price _____ Mileage _____

Purchased by _____

Make_____ Year_____ Model_____

Purchased from _____

Date of Purchase _____ Price _____ ID/VIN Number _____

Sales/ Trade Date_____ Price _____ Mileage _____

Purchased by _____

Make_____ Year_____ Model_____

Purchased from _____

Date of Purchase _____ Price _____ ID/VIN Number _____

Sales/ Trade Date_____ Price _____ Mileage _____

Purchased by _____

Make_____ Year_____ Model_____

Purchased from _____

_____

Date of Purchase _____ Price _____ ID/VIN Number_____

Sales/ Trade Date_____ Price _____ Mileage _____

Purchased by _____

Make_____ Year_____ Model_____

Purchased from _____

_____

Date of Purchase _____ Price _____ ID/VIN Number_____

Sales/ Trade Date_____ Price _____ Mileage _____

Purchased by _____

Make_____ Year_____ Model_____

Purchased from _____

_____

Date of Purchase _____ Price _____ ID/VIN Number_____

Sales/ Trade Date_____ Price _____ Mileage _____

Purchased by _____

Other Personal Property

Type_____ Make_____ ID Number _____

Purchase Date_____ Price_____ Sales Date_____ Price _____

Type_____ Make_____ ID Number _____

Purchase Date_____ Price_____ Sales Date_____ Price _____

Type_____ Make_____ ID Number _____

Purchase Date_____ Price_____ Sales Date_____ Price _____

Type_____ Make_____ ID Number _____

Purchase Date_____ Price_____ Sales Date_____ Price _____

Type_____ Make_____ ID Number _____

Purchase Date_____ Price_____ Sales Date_____ Price _____

Type_____ Make_____ ID Number _____

Purchase Date_____ Price_____ Sales Date_____ Price _____

Type_____ Make_____ ID Number _____

Purchase Date_____ Price_____ Sales Date_____ Price _____

Type_____ Make_____ ID Number _____

Purchase Date_____ Price_____ Sales Date_____ Price _____

Type_____ Make_____ ID Number _____

Purchase Date_____ Price_____ Sales Date_____ Price _____

Type_____ Make_____ ID Number _____

Purchase Date_____ Price_____ Sales Date_____ Price _____

Type_____ Make_____ ID Number _____

Purchase Date_____ Price_____ Sales Date_____ Price _____

Type_____ Make_____ ID Number _____

Purchase Date_____ Price_____ Sales Date_____ Price _____

Type_____ Make_____ ID Number _____

Purchase Date_____ Price_____ Sales Date_____ Price _____

Type_____ Make_____ ID Number _____

Purchase Date_____ Price_____ Sales Date_____ Price _____

Type_____ Make_____ ID Number _____

Purchase Date_____ Price_____ Sales Date_____ Price _____

Type_____ Make_____ ID Number _____

Purchase Date_____ Price_____ Sales Date_____ Price _____

Type_____ Make_____ ID Number _____

Purchase Date_____ Price_____ Sales Date_____ Price _____

Type_____ Make_____ ID Number _____

Purchase Date_____ Price_____ Sales Date_____ Price _____

Household Inventory

LIVING ROOM

Number of Items	Description of Items	Year Purchased	Original Cost	Estimate of Present Value	Date

DINING ROOM

Number of Items	Description of Items	Year Purchased	Original Cost	Estimate of Present Value	Date

LIBRARY, DEN OR STUDY

Number of Items	Description of Items	Year Purchased	Original Cost	Estimate of Present Value	Date

RECREATION OR FAMILY ROOM

Number of Items	Description of Items	Year Purchased	Original Cost	Estimate of Present Value	Date

HALLS, SUN-ROOMS AND PORCHES

Number of Items	Description of Items	Year Purchased	Original Cost	Estimate of Present Value	Date

BATHROOM(S)

Number of Items	Description of Items	Year Purchased	Original Cost	Estimate of Present Value	Date

BEDROOM(S)
including Sewing Room

Number of Items	Description of Items	Year Purchased	Original Cost	Estimate of Present Value	Date

KITCHEN
including Breakfast Room, Pantry and Laundry Room

Number of Items	Description of Items	Year Purchased	Original Cost	Estimate of Present Value	Date
Major Appliances					
Small Appliances					
Furniture					

ATTIC, BASEMENT AND GARAGE

Number of Items	Description of Items	Year Purchased	Original Cost	Estimate of Present Value	Date

JEWELRY

Don't forget valuable belts and hair ornaments.

Number of Items	Description of Items	Year Purchased	Original Cost	Estimate of Present Value	Date

FINE ARTS AND COLLECTIONS

including such valuable items as: paintings, antique
furniture, porcelain, statuary, coin collections, etc.

Number of Items	Description of Items	Year Purchased	Original Cost	Estimate of Present Value	Date

MUSICAL INSTRUMENTS AND ACCESSORIES

Number of Items	Description of Items	Year Purchased	Original Cost	Estimate of Present Value	Date

FURS
including all garments in which fur represents the principal value

Number of Items	Description of Items	Year Purchased	Original Cost	Estimate of Present Value	Date

SILVERWARE

Number of Items	Description of Items	Year Purchased	Original Cost	Estimate of Present Value	Date

CHINA AND GLASSWARE

Number of Items	Description of Items	Year Purchased	Original Cost	Estimate of Present Value	Date

SPORTS AND HOBBY EQUIPMENT

Number of Items	Description of Items	Year Purchased	Original Cost	Estimate of Present Value	Date

SUMMARY

	Total Orig. Cost	Date	Est. of Present Value	Date	Est. of Present Value
Living Room					
Dining Room					
Library, Den or Study					
Recreation or Family Room					
Halls, Sun-rooms and Porches					
Bathroom(s)					
Bedroom(s) including Sewing Room					
Kitchen, including Breakfast Room, Pantry and Laundry Room					
Attic, Basement and Garage					
Jewelry					
Furs, including all garments in which fur represents the principal value					
Fine Arts and Collections					
Musical Instruments and Accessories					
Silverware					
China and Glassware					
Sports and Hobby Equipment					
GRAND TOTAL					
Total Amount of Your Present Insurance on Personal Property:					

DID YOU REMEMBER?

air conditioners

bar equipment, including wines and liquors

clocks

decorative items

fireplace fixtures

floor coverings, including pads

lawn decorations

lawn furniture

valuable lighting fixtures

radios

sewing machines and equipment

tape equipment

televisions

typewriters

vacuum cleaners

window accessories

Safe Deposit Box

Valuables and documents subject to destruction by fire should be kept in a safe deposit box. However, if any such documents, such as your will or a funeral contract, must be readily available immediately on death, be sure to authorize access to that safe deposit box by your legal representative. Keep this section up-to-date by reviewing these records periodically.

Bank_____ Address_____

Date Opened_____ Key Location_____

In Name of _____

INVENTORY

_____

_____

_____

_____

_____

_____

_____

_____

_____

_____

_____

_____

_____

_____

Bank_____ Address _____

Date Opened_____ Key Location_____

In Name of _____

INVENTORY

_____

_____

_____

_____

_____

_____

_____

_____

_____

_____

_____

_____

_____

_____

_____

_____

_____

Bank_____ Address_____

Date Opened_____ Key Location_____

In Name of _____

INVENTORY

_____
_____
_____
_____
_____
_____
_____
_____
_____
_____
_____
_____
_____
_____
_____
_____
_____

Bank Accounts

Type _____

Bank and Address _____

_____

In Name of _____

Account Number _____ Date Opened-Closed _____

Type _____

Bank and Address _____

_____

In Name of _____

Account Number _____ Date Opened-Closed _____

Type _____

Bank and Address _____

_____

In Name of _____

Account Number _____ Date Opened-Closed _____

Type _____

Bank and Address _____

_____

In Name of _____

Account Number _____ Date Opened-Closed _____

Type _____

Bank and Address _____

_____

In Name of _____

Account Number _____ Date Opened-Closed _____

Type _____

Bank and Address _____

_____

In Name of _____

Account Number _____ Date Opened-Closed _____

Type _____

Bank and Address _____

_____

In Name of _____

Account Number _____ Date Opened-Closed _____

Type _____

Bank and Address _____

_____

In Name of _____

Account Number _____ Date Opened-Closed _____

Type _____

Bank and Address _____

_____

In Name of _____

Account Number _____ Date Opened-Closed _____

Type _____

Bank and Address _____

_____

In Name of _____

Account Number _____ Date Opened-Closed _____

Type _____

Bank and Address _____

_____

In Name of _____

Account Number _____ Date Opened-Closed _____

Insurance

Be sure to include coverage which is employer - provided, separately purchased, or provided through union, professional society, or alumnae association.

LIFE INSURANCE

Company _____ Type _____

Policy Number _____ Face Value _____

Beneficiary(s) _____

_____

Effective Date _____ Expiration Date _____

Premium _____

Where Policy Kept _____

Company _____ Type _____

Policy Number _____ Face Value _____

Beneficiary(s) _____

_____

Effective Date _____ Expiration Date _____

Premium _____

Where Policy Kept _____

ENDOWMENT AND ANNUITY INSURANCE

Company _____ Type _____

Policy Number _____ Value _____

Premium _____ Annual ☐ Semi-Annual ☐ Monthly ☐ Quarterly ☐

Option _____

Where Policy Kept _____

Company _____ Type _____

Policy Number _____ Value _____

Premium _____ Annual ☐ Semi-Annual ☐ Monthly ☐ Quarterly ☐

Option _____

Where Policy Kept _____

Company _____ Type _____

Policy Number _____ Value _____

Premium _____ Annual ☐ Semi-Annual ☐ Monthly ☐ Quarterly ☐

Option _____

Where Policy Kept _____

HOSPITALIZATION AND HEALTH INSURANCE

Company _____ Type _____

Policy Number _____

Coverage _____ Amount Deductible _____

Effective Date _____ Expiration Date _____

Premium _____

Where Policy Kept _____

Company _____ Type _____

Policy Number _____

Coverage _____ Amount Deductible _____

Effective Date _____ Expiration Date _____

Premium _____

Where Policy Kept _____

Company _____ Type _____

Policy Number _____

Coverage _____ Amount Deductible _____

Effective Date _____ Expiration Date _____

Premium _____

Where Policy Kept _____

REAL PROPERTY INSURANCE

Company_____ Type _____

Policy Number_____

Value _____ Amount Deductible _____

Effective Date_____ Expiration Date_____

Premium _____

Where Policy Kept _____

Company_____ Type _____

Policy Number_____

Value _____ Amount Deductible _____

Effective Date_____ Expiration Date_____

Premium _____

Where Policy Kept _____

Company_____ Type _____

Policy Number_____

Value _____ Amount Deductible _____

Effective Date_____ Expiration Date_____

Premium _____

Where Policy Kept _____

PERSONAL PROPERTY INSURANCE

Company _____ Type _____

Policy Number _____

Value _____ Amount Deductible _____

Effective Date _____ Expiration Date _____

Premium _____

Where Policy Kept _____

Company _____ Type _____

Policy Number _____

Value _____ Amount Deductible _____

Effective Date _____ Expiration Date _____

Premium _____

Where Policy Kept _____

Company _____ Type _____

Policy Number _____

Value _____ Amount Deductible _____

Effective Date _____ Expiration Date _____

Premium _____

Where Policy Kept _____

Other Insurance Information

Pension and Profit-Sharing Plan

Plan Name _____

Name and Address of Employer _____

_____

Employer ID Number _____ Plan Number _____

Type of Plan _____

When Vested _____

Type of Administration of Plan _____

Plan Administrator _____

Address _____

Telephone Number _____

Trustees (Name and Address) _____

_____

_____

_____

_____

_____

Benefits _____

_____

_____

Plan Name _____

Name and Address of Employer _____

_____

Employer ID Number _____ Plan Number _____

Type of Plan _____

When Vested _____

Type of Administration of Plan _____

Plan Administrator _____

Address _____

Telephone Number _____

Trustees (Name and Address) _____

_____

_____

_____

_____

_____

Benefits _____

_____

_____

Disability/Income Protection

Compensation _____ Type _____

Policy Number _____

Coverage _____

Where Policy Kept _____

_____

Compensation _____ Type _____

Policy Number _____

Coverage _____

Where Policy Kept _____

_____

Compensation _____ Type _____

Policy Number _____

Coverage _____

Where Policy Kept _____

_____

Credit Cards and Charge Accounts

CREDIT CARDS

Date _____

Name of Card or Company_____

Address _____

Card Number_____ Expiration Date_____

Date _____

Name of Card or Company_____

Address _____

Card Number_____ Expiration Date_____

Date _____

Name of Card or Company_____

Address _____

Card Number_____ Expiration Date_____

Date _____

Name of Card or Company_____

Address _____

Card Number_____ Expiration Date_____

Date _____

Name of Card or Company_____

Address _____

Card Number_____ Expiration Date_____

Date _____

Name of Card or Company_____

Address _____

Card Number_____ Expiration Date_____

Date _____

Name of Card or Company_____

Address _____

Card Number_____ Expiration Date_____

Date _____

Name of Card or Company_____

Address _____

Card Number_____ Expiration Date_____

Date _____

Name of Card or Company_____

Address _____

Card Number_____ Expiration Date_____

CHECK CASHING CARDS

Where Issued _____

Address _____

In Whose Name _____

Date _____

Number _____

Where Issued _____

Address _____

In Whose Name _____

Date _____

Number _____

Where Issued _____

Address _____

In Whose Name _____

Date _____

Number _____

Where Issued _____

Address _____

In Whose Name _____

Date _____

Number _____

Where Issued _____

Address _____

In Whose Name _____

Date _____

Number _____

Where Issued _____

Address _____

In Whose Name _____

Date _____

Number _____

Where Issued _____

Address _____

In Whose Name _____

Date _____

Number _____

Where Issued _____

Address _____

In Whose Name _____

Date _____

Number _____

STORE ACCOUNTS

Date _____

Name of Store _____

Address _____

Card Number _____ Expiration Date_____

Date _____

Name of Store _____

Address _____

Card Number _____ Expiration Date_____

Date _____

Name of Store _____

Address _____

Card Number _____ Expiration Date_____

Date _____

Name of Store _____

Address _____

Card Number _____ Expiration Date_____

Date _____

Name of Store _____

Address _____

Card Number _____ Expiration Date _____

Date _____

Name of Store _____

Address _____

Card Number _____ Expiration Date _____

Date _____

Name of Store _____

Address _____

Card Number _____ Expiration Date _____

Date _____

Name of Store _____

Address _____

Card Number _____ Expiration Date _____

Date _____

Name of Store _____

Address _____

Card Number _____ Expiration Date _____

Date _____

Name of Store _____

Address _____

Card Number _____ Expiration Date _____

Date _____

Name of Store _____

Address _____

Card Number _____ Expiration Date _____

Date _____

Name of Store _____

Address _____

Card Number _____ Expiration Date _____

Tax Records

Year _____

☐ Held by Attorney _____

_____

☐ Held by Accountant _____

_____

☐ Held by Self   Safe Deposit Box Number _____

Amount Paid _____
                        FEDERAL   STATE   CITY

Amount Refunded _____
                        FEDERAL   STATE   CITY

Other Information _____

Year _____

☐ Held by Attorney _____

_____

☐ Held by Accountant _____

_____

☐ Held by Self   Safe Deposit Box Number _____

Amount Paid _____
                        FEDERAL   STATE   CITY

Amount Refunded _____
                        FEDERAL   STATE   CITY

Other Information _____

Year_____

☐ Held by Attorney_____

_____

☐ Held by Accountant _____

_____

☐ Held by Self   Safe Deposit Box Number_____

Amount Paid _____
                           FEDERAL   STATE   CITY

Amount Refunded _____
                           FEDERAL   STATE   CITY

Other Information_____

Year_____

☐ Held by Attorney_____

_____

☐ Held by Accountant _____

_____

☐ Held by Self   Safe Deposit Box Number_____

Amount Paid _____
                           FEDERAL   STATE   CITY

Amount Refunded _____
                           FEDERAL   STATE   CITY

Other Information_____

Year_____

☐ Held by Attorney_____

_____

☐ Held by Accountant _____

_____

☐ Held by Self   Safe Deposit Box Number_____

Amount Paid _____
                     FEDERAL   STATE   CITY

Amount Refunded _____
                     FEDERAL   STATE   CITY

Other Information_____

Year_____

☐ Held by Attorney_____

_____

☐ Held by Accountant _____

_____

☐ Held by Self   Safe Deposit Box Number_____

Amount Paid _____
                     FEDERAL   STATE   CITY

Amount Refunded _____
                     FEDERAL   STATE   CITY

Other Information_____

Year_____

☐ Held by Attorney_____

_____

☐ Held by Accountant _____

_____

☐ Held by Self   Safe Deposit Box Number_____

Amount Paid _____
                        FEDERAL   STATE   CITY

Amount Refunded _____
                        FEDERAL   STATE   CITY

Other Information_____

Year_____

☐ Held by Attorney_____

_____

☐ Held by Accountant _____

_____

☐ Held by Self   Safe Deposit Box Number_____

Amount Paid _____
                        FEDERAL   STATE   CITY

Amount Refunded _____
                        FEDERAL   STATE   CITY

Other Information_____

Year_____

☐ Held by Attorney_____

_____

☐ Held by Accountant _____

_____

☐ Held by Self   Safe Deposit Box Number_____

Amount Paid _____
                        FEDERAL   STATE   CITY

Amount Refunded_____
                        FEDERAL   STATE   CITY

Other Information_____

Year_____

☐ Held by Attorney_____

_____

☐ Held by Accountant _____

_____

☐ Held by Self   Safe Deposit Box Number_____

Amount Paid _____
                        FEDERAL   STATE   CITY

Amount Refunded _____
                        FEDERAL   STATE   CITY

Other Information_____

Personal Property Tax

Year_____ Taxing Authority_____

Description of Property _____

Amount Paid _____ Date Paid_____

Year_____ Taxing Authority_____

Description of Property _____

Amount Paid _____ Date Paid_____

Year_____ Taxing Authority_____

Description of Property _____

Amount Paid _____ Date Paid_____

Year _____ Taxing Authority_____

Description of Property _____

Amount Paid _____ Date Paid_____

Year_____ Taxing Authority_____

Description of Property _____

Amount Paid _____ Date Paid_____

Year_____ Taxing Authority_____

Description of Property _____

Amount Paid _____ Date Paid_____

Year_____ Taxing Authority_____

Description of Property _____

Amount Paid _____ Date Paid_____

Year_____ Taxing Authority_____

Description of Property _____

Amount Paid _____ Date Paid_____

Year_____ Taxing Authority_____

Description of Property _____

Amount Paid _____ Date Paid_____

Year_____ Taxing Authority_____

Description of Property _____

Amount Paid _____ Date Paid_____

Year_____ Taxing Authority_____

Description of Property _____

Amount Paid _____ Date Paid_____

Year_____ Taxing Authority_____

Description of Property _____

Amount Paid _____ Date Paid_____

Year_____ Taxing Authority_____

Description of Property _____

Amount Paid _____ Date Paid_____

Year_____ Taxing Authority_____

Description of Property _____

Amount Paid _____ Date Paid_____

Year_____ Taxing Authority_____

Description of Property _____

Amount Paid _____ Date Paid_____

Excise and Other Taxes

Year_____ Taxing Authority_____

Nature of Tax _____

Amount Paid _____ Date Paid_____

Year_____ Taxing Authority_____

Nature of Tax _____

Amount Paid _____ Date Paid_____

Year_____ Taxing Authority_____

Nature of Tax _____

Amount Paid _____ Date Paid_____

Year_____ Taxing Authority_____

Nature of Tax _____

Amount Paid _____ Date Paid_____

Year_____ Taxing Authority_____

Nature of Tax _____

Amount Paid _____ Date Paid_____

Year_____ Taxing Authority_____

Nature of Tax _____

Amount Paid _____ Date Paid_____

Year_____ Taxing Authority_____

Nature of Tax _____

Amount Paid _____ Date Paid_____

Year_____ Taxing Authority_____

Nature of Tax _____

Amount Paid _____ Date Paid_____

Year_____ Taxing Authority_____

Nature of Tax _____

Amount Paid _____ Date Paid_____

Year_____ Taxing Authority_____

Nature of Tax _____

Amount Paid _____ Date Paid_____

Year_____ Taxing Authority_____

Nature of Tax _____

Amount Paid _____ Date Paid_____

Year_____ Taxing Authority_____

Nature of Tax _____

Amount Paid _____ Date Paid_____

Year_____ Taxing Authority_____

Nature of Tax _____

Amount Paid _____ Date Paid_____

Year_____ Taxing Authority_____

Nature of Tax _____

Amount Paid _____ Date Paid_____

Year_____ Taxing Authority_____

Nature of Tax _____

Amount Paid _____ Date Paid_____

Patents and Copyrights

Date of Application _____

Nature of Application _____

_____

Name and Address of Attorney _____

_____

Date of Registration _____

Date of Application _____

Nature of Application _____

_____

Name and Address of Attorney _____

_____

Date of Registration _____

Date of Application _____

Nature of Application _____

_____

Name and Address of Attorney _____

_____

Date of Registration _____

Additional Advisors
and Consultants

Additional Property Records

PART V

Miscellaneous Records and Lists

Important Names and Addresses

Name _____ Address _____

Telephone _____ _____

Name _____ Address _____

Telephone _____ _____

Name _____ Address _____

Telephone _____ _____

Name _____ Address _____

Telephone _____ _____

Name _____ Address _____

Telephone _____ _____

Name _____ Address _____

Telephone _____ _____

Name _____ Address _____

Telephone _____ _____

Name _____ Address _____

Telephone _____ _____

Name _____ Address _____

Telephone _____ _____

Name _____ Address _____

Telephone _____ _____

Name _____ Address _____

Telephone _____ _____

Name _____ Address _____

Telephone _____ _____

Name _____ Address _____

Telephone _____ _____

Name _____ Address _____

Telephone _____ _____

Name _____ Address _____

Telephone _____ _____

Name _____ Address _____

Telephone _____ _____

Name _____ Address _____

Telephone _____ _____

Name _____ Address _____

Telephone _____ _____

Name _____ Address _____

Telephone _____ _____

Name _____ Address _____

Telephone _____ _____

Name _____ Addresss _____

Telephone _____ _____

Name _____ Address _____

Telephone _____ _____

Name _____ Address _____

Telephone _____ _____

Name _____ Address _____

Telephone _____ _____

Name _____ Address _____

Telephone _____ _____

Name _____ Address _____

Telephone _____ _____

Birthdays

Name   Date

_____   _____

_____   _____

_____   _____

_____   _____

_____   _____

_____   _____

_____   _____

_____   _____

_____   _____

_____   _____

_____   _____

_____   _____

_____   _____

_____   _____

_____   _____

Name

Date

Anniversaries

Name

Date

Name   Date

_____   _____

_____   _____

_____   _____

_____   _____

_____   _____

_____   _____

_____   _____

_____   _____

_____   _____

_____   _____

_____   _____

_____   _____

_____   _____

_____   _____

_____   _____

_____   _____

_____   _____

Graduations

Name	Occasion	Date

Name	Occasion	Date

Christmas Card List

Year_____ Name _____

Address _____

Year_____ Name _____

Address _____

Year_____ Name _____

Address _____

Year_____ Name _____

Address _____

Year_____ Name _____

Address _____

Year_____ Name _____

Address _____

Year_____ Name _____

Address _____

Year_____ Name _____

Address _____

Year_____ Name _____

Address _____

Year_____ Name _____

Address _____

Year_____ Name _____

Address _____

Year_____ Name _____

Address _____

Year_____ Name _____

Address _____

Year_____ Name _____

Address _____

Year_____ Name _____

Address _____

Year_____ Name _____

Address _____

Year_____ Name _____

Address _____

Year _____ Name _____

Address _____

Year _____ Name _____

Address _____

Year _____ Name _____

Address _____

Year _____ Name _____

Address _____

Year _____ Name _____

Address _____

Year _____ Name _____

Address _____

Year _____ Name _____

Address _____

Year _____ Name _____

Address _____

Year _____ Name _____

Address _____

Year _____ Name _____

Address _____

Year _____ Name _____

Address _____

Year _____ Name _____

Address _____

Year _____ Name _____

Address _____

Year _____ Name _____

Address _____

Year _____ Name _____

Address _____

Year _____ Name _____

Address _____

Year _____ Name _____

Address _____

Year _____ Name _____

Address _____

Year_____ Name _____

Address _____

Year_____ Name _____

Address _____

Year_____ Name _____

Address _____

Year_____ Name _____

Address _____

Year_____ Name _____

Address _____

Year_____ Name _____

Address _____

Year_____ Name _____

Address _____

Year_____ Name _____

Address _____

Year_____ Name _____

Address _____

Year_____ Name _____

Address _____

Year_____ Name _____

Address _____

Year_____ Name _____

Address _____

Year_____ Name _____

Address _____

Year_____ Name _____

Address _____

Year_____ Name _____

Address _____

Year_____ Name _____

Address _____

Year_____ Name _____

Address _____

Year_____ Name _____

Address _____

Year_____ Name _____

Address _____

Year_____ Name _____

Address _____

Year_____ Name _____

Address _____

Year_____ Name _____

Address _____

Year_____ Name _____

Address _____

Year_____ Name _____

Address _____

Year_____ Name _____

Address _____

Year_____ Name _____

Address _____

Year_____ Name _____

Address _____

Year_____ Name _____

Address _____

Year_____ Name _____

Address _____

Year_____ Name _____

Address _____

Year_____ Name _____

Address _____

Year_____ Name _____

Address _____

Year_____ Name _____

Address _____

Year_____ Name _____

Address _____

Year_____ Name _____

Address _____

Year_____ Name _____

Address _____

Gifts Given

To _____ Date _____

Occasion _____ Item_____

To _____ Date _____

Occasion _____ Item_____

To _____ Date _____

Occasion _____ Item_____

To _____ Date _____

Occasion _____ Item_____

To _____ Date _____

Occasion _____ Item_____

To _____ Date _____

Occasion _____ Item_____

To _____ Date _____

Occasion _____ Item_____

To _____ Date _____

Occasion _____ Item_____

To _____ Date _____

Occasion _____ Item_____

To _____ Date _____

Occasion _____ Item_____

To _____ Date _____

Occasion _____ Item_____

To _____ Date _____

Occasion _____ Item_____

To _____ Date _____

Occasion _____ Item_____

To _____ Date _____

Occasion _____ Item_____

To _____ Date _____

Occasion _____ Item_____

To _____ Date _____

Occasion _____ Item_____

To _____ Date _____

Occasion _____ Item_____

To _____ Date _____

Occasion _____ Item _____

To _____ Date _____

Occasion _____ Item _____

To _____ Date _____

Occasion _____ Item _____

To _____ Date _____

Occasion _____ Item _____

To _____ Date _____

Occasion _____ Item _____

To _____ Date _____

Occasion _____ Item _____

To _____ Date _____

Occasion _____ Item _____

To _____ Date _____

Occasion _____ Item _____

To _____ Date _____

Occasion _____ Item _____

Gifts Received

From _____ Date _____

Occasion _____ Item _____

From _____ Date _____

Occasion _____ Item _____

From _____ Date _____

Occasion _____ Item _____

From _____ Date _____

Occasion _____ Item _____

From _____ Date _____

Occasion _____ Item _____

From _____ Date _____

Occasion _____ Item _____

From _____ Date _____

Occasion _____ Item _____

From _____ Date _____

Occasion _____ Item _____

From _____ Date _____

Occasion _____ Item _____

From _____ Date _____

Occasion _____ Item _____

From _____ Date _____

Occasion _____ Item _____

From _____ Date _____

Occasion _____ Item _____

From _____ Date _____

Occasion _____ Item _____

From _____ Date _____

Occasion _____ Item _____

From _____ Date _____

Occasion _____ Item _____

From _____ Date _____

Occasion _____ Item _____

From _____ Date _____

Occasion _____ Item _____

From _____ Date _____

Occasion _____ Item_____

From _____ Date _____

Occasion _____ Item_____

From _____ Date _____

Occasion _____ Item_____

From _____ Date _____

Occasion _____ Item_____

From _____ Date _____

Occasion _____ Item_____

From _____ Date _____

Occasion _____ Item_____

From _____ Date _____

Occasion _____ Item_____

From _____ Date _____

Occasion _____ Item_____

From _____ Date _____

Occasion _____ Item_____

Memorable Family Events

Date _____ Occasion _____

Guests _____ Menu _____

_____ _____

_____ _____

_____ _____

_____ _____

_____ _____

_____ _____

Date _____ Occasion _____

Guests _____ Menu _____

_____ _____

_____ _____

_____ _____

_____ _____

_____ _____

Date _____ Occasion _____

Guests _____ Menu _____

_____ _____

_____ _____

_____ _____

_____ _____

_____ _____

_____ _____

Date _____ Occasion _____

Guests _____ Menu _____

_____ _____

_____ _____

_____ _____

_____ _____

_____ _____

Date _____ Occasion _____

Guests _____ Menu _____

_____ _____

_____ _____

_____ _____

_____ _____

_____ _____

_____ _____

_____ _____

Date _____ Occasion _____

Guests _____ Menu _____

_____ _____

_____ _____

_____ _____

_____ _____

_____ _____

_____ _____

Date _____ Occasion _____

Guests _____ Menu _____

_____ _____

_____ _____

_____ _____

_____ _____

_____ _____

_____ _____

_____ _____

Date _____ Occasion _____

Guests _____ Menu _____

_____ _____

_____ _____

_____ _____

_____ _____

_____ _____

_____ _____

Pets

Name _____ Breed _____ Date Acquired _____

Age When Acquired_____ Date of Death _____ Age at Death_____

Name _____ Breed _____ Date Acquired _____

Age When Acquired_____ Date of Death _____ Age at Death_____

Name _____ Breed _____ Date Acquired _____

Age When Acquired_____ Date of Death _____ Age at Death_____

Name _____ Breed _____ Date Acquired _____

Age When Acquired_____ Date of Death _____ Age at Death_____

Name _____ Breed _____ Date Acquired _____

Age When Acquired_____ Date of Death _____ Age at Death_____

Name _____ Breed _____ Date Acquired _____

Age When Acquired_____ Date of Death _____ Age at Death_____

Name _____ Breed _____ Date Acquired _____

Age When Acquired_____ Date of Death _____ Age at Death_____

Name _____ Breed _____ Date Acquired _____

Age When Acquired_____ Date of Death _____ Age at Death_____

Travel Records

Dates From-To _____ Place _____

Accomodations _____

_____

Travel Agent _____

Costs _____

Remarks _____

_____

_____

Dates From-To _____ Place _____

Accomodations _____

_____

Travel Agent _____

Costs _____

Remarks _____

_____

_____

Dates From-To _____ Place _____

Accomodations_____

_____

Travel Agent_____

Costs_____

Remarks_____

Dates From-To _____ Place _____

Accomodations_____

_____

Travel Agent_____

Costs_____

Remarks_____

Dates From-To _____ Place _____

Accomodations_____

_____

Travel Agent_____

Costs_____

Remarks_____

Dates From-To _____ Place _____

Accomodations _____

_____

Travel Agent _____

Costs _____

Remarks _____

Dates From-To _____ Place _____

Accomodations _____

_____

Travel Agent _____

Costs _____

Remarks _____

Dates From-To _____ Place _____

Accomodations _____

_____

Travel Agent _____

Costs _____

Remarks _____

Dates From-To _____ Place _____

Accomodations_____

_____

Travel Agent_____

Costs_____

Remarks_____

Dates From-To _____ Place _____

Accomodations_____

_____

Travel Agent_____

Costs_____

Remarks_____

Dates From-To _____ Place _____

Accomodations_____

_____

Travel Agent_____

Costs_____

Remarks_____

Dates From-To _____ Place _____

Accomodations _____

_____

Travel Agent _____

Costs _____

Remarks _____

Dates From-To _____ Place _____

Accomodations _____

_____

Travel Agent _____

Costs _____

Remarks _____

Dates From-To _____ Place _____

Accomodations _____

_____

Travel Agent _____

Costs _____

Remarks _____

Additional Record Space

Additional Record Space

Additional Record Space

Additional Record Space

Additional Record Space

Additional Record Space

Additional Record Space

Additional Record Space